"Noah, about that kiss…"

She swung toward him as they strode across a little bridge that arced over a tiny tributary of the river, the water in it reflecting the city lights. "I know I took you off guard and probably shocked you, and weirded you out and stuff. In hindsight I shouldn't have done it. I should've done what you were doing and just faced them down, but I panicked and—"

"I wasn't weirded out, Bree."

Her eyes looked huge in the moonlight. "You weren't?"

Her voice sounded small and a little forlorn, and it caught at him. "The thing is, Bree, what I really wanted to do was kiss you back."

Her eyes grew even bigger and rounder. But the expression in them was neither shocked nor appalled.

His hand went to either side of her on the railing, and he couldn't find it in him to regret his honesty. "What I really want to do is kiss you now."

Dear Reader,

Road trip stories have always fascinated me. The image of the wide-open road seems so romantically full of potential. Then there are the unexpected delays and detours that inevitably occur along the way. Best of all, though, are the sparks that fly when two people are trapped by circumstances and forced to spend all of that time alone together in the confines of a car. Add to that the sensation of having stepped outside of the normal boundaries of life and one has all of the ingredients for the trip of a lifetime.

Bree and Noah's road trip is often fraught, frequently funny and very emotional. These two care deeply for each other and come to care even more as they start to gain a new appreciation for one another. But the stakes are high, which makes for an uncomfortable, confronting, but also exhilarating experience as they embark on a journey of two thousand and five hundred kilometers together. I hope you cheer for Bree and Noah as much as I did as they fight for the happy-ever-after they never knew they wanted or needed.

Hugs and happy reading!

Michelle

Billionaire's Road Trip to Forever

—

Michelle Douglas

Recycling programs for this product may not exist in your area.

ISBN-13: 978-1-335-40673-6

Billionaire's Road Trip to Forever

Harlequin Enterprises ULC
22 Adelaide St. West, 40th Floor
Toronto, Ontario M5H 4E3, Canada
www.Harlequin.com

Printed in U.S.A.

Michelle Douglas has been writing for Harlequin since 2007 and believes she has the best job in the world. She lives in a leafy suburb of Newcastle, on Australia's east coast, with her own romantic hero, a house full of dust and books, and an eclectic collection of '60s and '70s vinyl. She loves to hear from readers and can be contacted via her website, michelle-douglas.com.

Books by Michelle Douglas

Harlequin Romance

A Baby in His In-Tray
The Million Pound Marriage Deal
Miss Prim's Greek Island Fling
The Maid, the Millionaire and the Baby
Redemption of the Maverick Millionaire
Singapore Fling with the Millionaire
Secret Billionaire on Her Doorstep

Visit the Author Profile page
at Harlequin.com for more titles.

To Greg, the best lockdown companion in the world! Thanks for the jigsaws, for always being able to make me laugh and for managing to keep us in essentials. There's no one I'd rather be in lockdown with.

Praise for
Michelle Douglas

"Michelle Douglas writes the most beautiful stories, with heroes and heroines who are real and so easy to get to know and love.... This is a moving and wonderful story that left me feeling fabulous.... I do highly recommend this one. Ms. Douglas has never disappointed me with her stories."

—*Goodreads* on *Redemption of the Maverick Millionaire*

CHAPTER ONE

THEY WERE THROUGH the 'dearly beloveds' and on to the 'if any person can show just cause why they may not be lawfully joined together' part of the marriage service, and just for a moment Bree's heart beat a little harder and faster in the hushed silence of Brisbane's Anglican cathedral. Well, as hushed as the crowded pews for the society wedding of the year would allow.

Noah might be about to make a mistake of monolithic proportions in marrying Courtney Fraser, but it was a little late to be standing up and pointing that out.

Could you imagine everyone's faces if she did, though?

She barely managed to suppress a shudder at the thought, but she couldn't suppress a sigh. Not that she had any real reason to object to the marriage, just gut instinct. And she doubted the Anglican minister officiating would consider that as 'just cause'.

Deep breaths, Bree. Paste on a smile.

It was just…seeing Noah about to make such a huge mistake had everything inside her protesting. She'd known Noah since she was a bratty eight-year-old. He was her twin brothers' best friend. She no more wanted to see him make such a mistake than she would them.

She glared at Blake's and Ryder's backs now. They were Noah's groomsmen—they had responsibilities! Why hadn't they taken Noah aside and talked sense into him…or at least grilled him to make sure this was what he really wanted?

She blew out a silent breath when nobody stood up to make a *Jane Eyre*-esque pronouncement to call a halt to the wedding. She pressed her hands together and hauled in a breath. Given the current divorce statistics, this marriage wouldn't be an irreversible mistake.

Oh, but what a wealth of pain and upheaval a divorce would cause all concerned. She wanted to weep at the thought of it.

'Stop fidgeting,' her mother murmured. 'You're making me nervous.'

Enough, she berated herself. It was time to stop being Miss Doom-and-Gloom, time to stop thinking such ugly thoughts. It wasn't as if she were a relationship expert or anything. Maybe Noah and Courtney would have a gloriously long and happy marriage and bless the day they'd met forever. She hoped so. Noah deserved to be happy.

Bree lifted her gaze from the *happy couple* to the stained-glass window and zoned out. In roughly five hours, as soon as she could politely and legitimately absent herself from the afternoon reception, she'd be on the first leg of her road trip—a road trip that was going to utterly change her entire life.

Her fingers started to ache and she glanced down to find them clenched in her lap. She flexed them, and swallowed. It was *normal* to find change a bit intimidating, right?

What about downright terrifying?

She dragged her attention back to the service in time to see the bride—an utter vision in white—push back her veil. 'I need to speak to you—' she pointed to the minister and then the bridal party '—in the vestry. *Now.*'

Bree blinked. *Say what?* Courtney had kept her voice low, but it still carried to the second pew where Bree sat.

The minister hesitated for two beats before silently gesturing for the bride to precede him to the small room off to the right. The rest of the bridal party followed with varying expressions of bewilderment and concern. Bree couldn't see Noah's face, but the tight set of his shoulders and uncompromising line of his back made her wince.

A murmur that all too quickly became a quiet roar went around the church. Bree exchanged glances with her parents, but they each remained silent. Nearly five minutes passed before a stern-faced Ryder stalked out and…

Dear God. Her brother was making directly for her.

'Bree, you're needed.' His eyes burned into hers trying to send her some secret message. 'Can you…?'

She rose and followed only because she couldn't think of an excuse to refuse. Not for the first time, she wished she hadn't come to the wedding, wished she'd made her excuses. Except this was Noah. She couldn't *not* attend Noah's wedding.

It felt as if every eye in the church—and there must've been over two hundred sets of them—was on her as she made what felt like the mile-long journey to the vestry. She supposed it would be awfully poor form to bolt out through the side door and get an early start on her road trip. Change might be scary, but *this*? Ooh, she had a feeling *this* was going to be truly awful.

Or not. Maybe this was just a minor hiccup.

The tension in the vestry squeezed her chest tight. Noah's pallor and the way he clenched his jaw had her own jaw aching in sympathy. As soon as Ryder closed the door behind them, Courtney swung to her. '*You* don't think I ought to marry Noah, do you?'

Whoa. Wait! *What?*

'That's why you refused to be my bridesmaid.'

Courtney was going to dump Noah. *At the altar?* It took what felt like a full minute to find her voice. 'I politely declined your request to be bridesmaid because nobody wants to be paired in a bridal party with one of their brothers. But more importantly,' she added when Courtney snorted—it was the oddest thing to hear such an inelegant sound emerge from an archetypal vision of bridal loveliness. 'More importantly,' she forced herself to continue, 'I'm Noah's friend, not yours.

'I mean, I'm sure we could be friends,' she added with unholy haste. In another dimension, perhaps. Or in a galaxy far, far away. 'But I'm of the firm belief that, on the wedding day, the bridesmaids should be there for the bride and only the bride, not as some kind of support or sop to the groom.'

For the entire time she spoke, Bree could feel the force and weight of Noah's gaze—as if by sheer force of will he could compel her to make things right. She didn't want to let him down. But she couldn't make things right until she knew what on earth was wrong.

'Why didn't you tell me that in the first place, then, instead of blathering on that you weren't sure you'd have the time or if you were even going to be in town for the wedding?'

She lifted a reluctant shoulder. 'I thought it sounded politer than the truth,' she mumbled. 'Besides, I had a feeling you only asked me to make Noah happy and, excuse me, but I'm always going to pass on playing the role of the pity bridesmaid.'

Courtney inclined her head as if acknowledging a hit. 'You still haven't answered my original question, though. You don't think I should marry Noah, do you?'

It was Bree's turn to snort, and she made sure it was twice as inelegant as Courtney's. 'No way am I weighing in on that. No one can make that decision except you and Noah.'

What was Courtney trying to do—turn Bree into the bad guy here? She'd pass on that role too, thank you very much.

'Why the hell are you having second thoughts *now*?' Noah ground out, his eyes blazing in the pallor of his face.

Bree winced. His every muscle was clenched so tight he shook. It made him look angry, belligerent, but she knew better. All of that mad tension hid panic…and probably a world of pain.

The finger he pointed at Courtney shook. 'I asked you to marry me *over a year ago*. You said yes *over a year ago*. You've had *over a year* to change your mind.'

He dragged a hand down his face and Bree's heart throbbed. Courtney couldn't do this to him. She just couldn't.

With what looked like a superhuman effort, he lifted his head. 'Look, wedding jitters are normal but…'

Courtney folded her arms over her tightly laced bodice. 'But?'

'But this is crazy. And don't you think it's a bit…overdramatic?'

He spread his hands as he spoke, but something inside Bree froze as she stared into his face. Her stomach tightened, and she backed up until she was out of the circle. She scrutinised his face and then Courtney's and slowly lowered herself to a chair.

Courtney's laugh held a note of hysteria. 'What if we're making a mistake? Doesn't that worry you?'

Bree's heart caught. Was she the only one who could see the sudden vulnerability in those china-blue eyes? Or was everyone else blinded by the vision of picture-perfect bridal perfection?

'We can talk about this later,' Noah hissed.
'We have over two hundred guests out there who
are waiting to see us get married.' His hands
clenched. 'Not to mention the press. The wedding reception is booked and a veritable feast
awaiting, not to mention the plan for the honeymoon. I don't know what else you want me to do.
I've agreed to *everything* you wanted.'

It was only because she knew him so well
that Bree recognised how he bit back the expletive chafing through him. Silently she said it for
him, *Courtney, he's agreed to every* damn *thing
you wanted.*

He went on to name all the manifold delights
they had waiting to share with their guests at the
wedding reception, and the secret European location they'd chosen for their honeymoon and had
so been looking forward to. He listed the myriad things they had to look forward to in their
shared life when they returned home from their
honeymoon. A shared life full of potential, purpose and privilege.

He spoke of holiday houses in Palm Springs
and an apartment in Sydney, named the best
grammar schools for the three children they
planned to have, mentioned the awards and accolades they'd win in their glittering and magnificent careers. 'Courtney, sweetheart—' he spread

his hands, his expression bewildered '—this is dream-come-true stuff.'

Bree swallowed the sigh welling through her. He made it sound amazing.

'We've talked and talked about this,' he continued, 'planned everything down to the smallest detail. I have every intention of doing all I can to make every single one of your dreams come true. Why have second thoughts now?'

It sounded like the most amazing dream.

Except for one thing.

He spread his arms wide. 'What have I missed? What else do you want?'

'Oh, yes! *You're* giving *me* so much.' Courtney threw up her arms. 'And what do *you* get in return?'

He stared. 'I get to marry you. I get the life I just described. What more *could* I want?'

Bree leaned forward on her chair, suddenly and achingly hyperaware. Say it, she urged silently. *Say it.*

'I get to be married to the smartest, most beautiful woman I know. A woman I never in a million years imagined would ever marry me.'

'I'm not some damn trophy you get to hold aloft, Noah!'

His mouth opened and closed but not a single word emerged.

Bree waited, her heart thumping. But still he

didn't say it. For the briefest of moments her and Courtney's gazes collided. Courtney kinked an eyebrow and Bree found herself slumping.

Noah *didn't* love Courtney.

And Courtney had only just realised that.

Bree couldn't blame the other woman for running as fast from Noah as she could. But why the heck couldn't she have come to this decision last week? Or even yesterday?

Courtney pressed her fingers to her temples. 'Noah, let's postpone the wedding so we can talk…work through a few things.' She dragged in a breath so shaky it made Bree think she was only holding it together by a thread.

The expression on Noah's face told them all what he thought about that idea.

Courtney's throat bobbed as she swallowed, her hands tightly clenched at her waist. 'It's just a delay. If you really love me…?'

Two beats of silence passed.

'Or, how's this for a plan?' Noah widened his stance. 'We get married right now.' He pointed back the way they'd come. 'We have a church full of guests, the caterers are booked, and everything is in place for your whole damn dream wedding.'

Courtney's eyes flashed. 'But it's not your whole damn dream wedding.'

'I don't care about the wedding. I just want to marry you!'

'Fine, marry me in a month, then!'

A terrifying smile stole across Noah's lips then and Bree's heart clenched at the self-loathing she recognised in his eyes, though she wondered if anyone else recognised it as such.

'If *you* loved *me*…' His lips twisted into a bitter smile. 'Here are the options, Courtney. Marry me now…'

'Or?'

'Don't marry me at all.'

Bree closed her eyes. A man in love didn't give those kinds of ultimatums.

Courtney's lips twisted. 'My dream wedding perhaps, but not my dream groom. I'm sorry, Noah, but I can't marry you.'

He'd gone so pale it made Bree's stomach churn. He could fix this so easily.

All he had to do was tell Courtney he loved her!

But the fact that saying the words didn't even occur to him spoke volumes. She wanted to drop her head to her hands. What a God-awful mess.

To Noah's credit, he didn't beg. He kept his chin high and his eyes hard. 'You're certain about this?'

'A hundred per cent.'

'And let me guess—' his nostrils flared '—

you're going to walk out and leave me to clean up the mess?'

Courtney hesitated, before turning to the minister. 'Are any of the wedding party required to go out there and explain that the wedding has been cancelled?'

'Absolutely not. In fact, I can do it with far less fuss and uproar than anyone else. And to be frank, I'd rather my church not be turned into a circus.'

Noah's lips twisted. 'The press are going to have a field day with this.'

'Then I'm leaving through the side door now.' Courtney picked up her skirts. 'I'm sorry to do this to you, Noah, but it really is for the best.'

'Wait.' Bree found herself on her feet. 'I have a bit of a plan. We all know the two of you are going to be pursued by the media.' Not just pursued, but probably hounded. 'Why don't the two of you leave—?'

'Separately,' Courtney snapped.

'That message has been received loud and clear,' Noah bit out through white lips.

Bree swallowed and started again. 'While you two slip away, separately, the rest of the bridal party can assemble back out there—' she hitched her head in the direction of the church '—as if the wedding is going to go ahead. It'll buy you both a little time to leave the church unhindered.'

Noah drew himself up to his full height of six feet one inch and the coldness in his eyes sent a shiver down Bree's spine. 'I'm not a coward, Bree. Courtney might be happy to make her little announcement and dash away, but I'm more than capable of going out there and facing the music, even if she isn't.'

Ooh, really bad idea. Especially when he was this angry. One look at his face and nobody in the church would blame Courtney for bolting. The press would go to town on him.

If Noah chose to annihilate Courtney's character in public, Bree wanted him to make the decision with a clear head, not this *fury*. She moistened her lips. 'It's not about being capable, Noah. It's about not feeding a media frenzy.'

'She's right, dude,' Ryder said. 'The two of you either go out there to make the announcement together or not at all.'

Courtney's eyes widened. '*I'm* not going out there.'

Ryder's lips twisted. 'Which is exactly what I'd expect of you...*now*.'

'Back off, hotshot!'

Hallelujah. The maid of honour could actually speak. Bree felt as if the only one doing any talking besides the bride and groom had been her.

'Why should it be your face that's splashed across the newspapers in the morning or on the TV this evening?' Bree said over the rising tide of voices. 'Let them drag out an old picture of the two of you and speculate to their hearts' content. You don't owe them anything.'

'And who'll cancel everything that needs cancelling?' Noah demanded.

'Goldilocks here and I will take care of all that.' Ryder gestured towards the maid of honour. 'You don't have to worry about a thing.'

She saw the exact moment Noah registered that whatever he did in the next few minutes would have repercussions on the company he and Ryder had built from the ground up. He could wilfully destroy his own reputation—and the company's—or he could go into damage control.

'I agree with your friends,' the minister said. 'This is the wisest course of action.'

Noah swore, making them all flinch.

'Do you have your car keys?' Ryder shot at Bree.

She nodded, blessing the fact she'd brought her clutch purse with her to the vestry and hadn't left it on the seat beside her mother.

'Take him straight to Mum and Dad's.'

Her? Why her?

'Whatever you do, don't take him to his apartment. The press will be swarming all over the place in an hour.'

Well, *doh*. But—

'Blake and I will try and delay them for as long as we can.'

Damn. Her brothers still had a role to play in all of this. One glance at Noah's pinched lips and the dangerous glitter in his eyes and she knew she couldn't let him go off by himself. Heaven only knew what he'd do.

'Go now,' Ryder whispered in her ear, pushing her in the direction of the door.

Refusing to give herself any time to think, she grabbed Noah's arm and towed him through the side entrance. Beneath the material of his tux, his arm was rock-solid muscle. Unbidden, a little shiver shook through her. Did Courtney know what she was doing, what she was giving up?

The woman was an idiot on so many levels. And yet Bree couldn't blame her for refusing to marry a man who didn't love her.

'Are you pleased with yourself?' Noah snarled as she drove her hatchback away from the church.

Uh-huh. Male logic at its best, no doubt. She understood his need to lash out, though. And as she was the only one currently available…

'Ecstatic,' she murmured, doing her best to keep her attention on the road rather than the bristling hulk of masculinity beside her. They said a woman scorned was a scary proposition, but perhaps they'd never seen a jilted groom. Bree would put them on a par.

'You had it in your power to convince Courtney to marry me and yet you refused to do it. Why would you serve me such a bad turn?' His brow pleated. 'Hell, Bree, I thought we were friends.'

His words cut her to her marrow, and she ran an orange light. 'Of course we're friends.'

'Then why would you destroy all my chances of happiness? You knew marrying Courtney is the only thing I've ever wanted.'

Her hands tightened on the steering wheel. 'I know you're feeling bad at the moment, Noah—hurt, angry, betrayed. But I refuse to take the blame for this. If you couldn't convince her to marry you, I don't see what hope you think I had.'

'All you had to say was that you thought we were well suited!' His voice rose. 'All you had to do was tell her we should *get married*!'

'You wanted me to lie?' They weren't the words she meant to say, but they were the ones that burst from her mouth.

'This is what it looks like at your apartment complex at the moment.'

Ryder handed Noah his phone and Noah grimaced. Talk about a media circus.

He closed his eyes. Everything ached. His temples pounded. His jaw throbbed. His throat burned with the effort of holding back all the ugly words he wanted to spew forth. His hands and shoulders ached at how tightly he clenched the one and braced the other.

And inside his chest an ugly gaping darkness lay in wait to claim him.

'Believe me, you don't want to go back there at the moment.'

'What's it like at yours?' he asked, handing back the phone. Ryder was his business partner and best man. His friend would be considered fair game—guilty by association—and Noah hated to have brought this furore to his friend's door as well.

'It's being staked out by a few hacks but nothing on this scale.'

But if Noah showed his face there… He shook his head. He wasn't bringing the slathering hordes to Ryder's doorstep.

'You can couch surf at mine,' Blake offered.

Blake shared the ultimate bachelor pad with two of the firefighters he worked with—but there was no room there, there'd be no privacy…and he couldn't face all the false jollification they'd rally for his benefit.

He understood it. He appreciated it. But he couldn't face it.

'Nonsense,' Janice Allenby said. 'You're staying here with us, Noah. We have plenty of room and we'd love to have you.'

A little gentle non-intrusive mothering from Mrs A would certainly help soothe the savage beast, but neither she nor her husband, Colin, needed the hassle of the media camped outside their front door. Janice was a high-profile public servant while Colin was a well-respected ophthalmologist. They were busy, hardworking people and he wasn't repaying their unremitting kindness with that.

It would kill him if they ever came to regret taking him under their wings. They'd all but adopted him when he'd moved to the area as an eleven-year-old—had even had brief custodial stints when his parents had been…otherwise occupied.

'Or,' Bree put in and then stopped.

They hadn't spoken since their harsh words in the car. He owed her an apology. And maybe she owed him one as well. He frowned. He wasn't sure about that, though. Maybe she'd had every right to say what she'd said.

Whatever the rights and wrongs of the case were, she'd brought him inside, rustled him up a pair of jeans and long-sleeved T, before sitting him at the kitchen table and handing him a beer. She'd sat on the other side of the table sipping a soda. It had been weirdly soothing—a bubble of quiet—before the rest of the Allenbys had raced in and the bubble had burst.

He dragged a hand down his face, suddenly feeling a hundred years old. When had everything become so complicated? When had it all gone to hell in a hand basket? How the hell had he not seen what had happened today coming?

He'd not had a single inkling that anything was wrong. Courtney's pronouncement had totally blindsided him. Just when he'd thought he was about to get everything he'd ever wanted.

When he pulled his hand back to his side and glanced up, something in Bree's eyes—the same colour as the milk chocolate she loved—gentled. 'Or,' she repeated, glancing at her watch, 'I'm leaving on my road trip in two hours.'

Very slowly, he straightened. What was she saying?

She dragged in a breath as if to bolster her resolve. 'You're welcome to tag along if you want.'

She shook her head and then rolled her eyes towards the ceiling as if she couldn't believe she'd just made the offer.

He frowned. 'Thanks, Bree, but I don't think—'

'Hold on a moment! *Think* about it.' Ryder swung to Noah, punching a fist into his hand. 'It could be the perfect solution. It's the last thing anyone would expect and, therefore, the last place anyone would think to look for you.'

Her father wrapped an arm around Bree's shoulders. 'Nice thinking, sweetie.'

It touched him the way the Allenby family wanted to protect him from the fallout of today's debacle. He couldn't avoid it forever, they all knew that—eventually he and Courtney would have to make some kind of public statement—but they'd do all they could to buy him some breathing space first.

And they were right. He needed a time out. His brain had shut down and he couldn't make sense of anything. God only knew what he'd say if cornered by the press at the moment.

And for the sake of his and Ryder's company, Fitness Ark, he couldn't afford to make a statement before thinking through what he was going to say very carefully first.

'It'd ease my mind to know Bree wasn't travelling alone,' Janice said.

'Mum.' Bree rolled her eyes again.

Blake shrugged. 'At least it'll give you someone to share the driving with.'

'As I'm not driving longer than six hours on any given day, that won't make much difference.'

'Ah, but with the two of you, you'll be able to go further faster,' Ryder said.

'I don't want to go further faster. I want to

take my time.' She glared at Noah as if he'd just agreed with her brother. 'And I'm not changing my mind about that.'

This trip of hers—a road trip to Tasmania—was mighty mysterious. Not to mention out of character. Sure, Bree had flown to Hobart several times over the last few years to visit her best friend, Tina. But that had only been for the odd long weekend.

Why drive when she could fly? Why would someone who was always on the move suddenly decide she needed to slow down?

Whenever questioned Bree just said the road trip was the break she needed before knuckling back down to work and thinking about the next phase of her life.

Due to The Plan, they all knew the next phase of Bree's life consisted of starting up her own physiotherapy practice. She'd been working hard towards that goal for the last seven years.

Still, a month-long road trip to Tasmania seemed too…random.

Why hadn't she chosen two weeks on a beach in Barbados? Or a month in Italy and France? She was up to something—and he knew he was using it as a displacement activity to take his mind off what had happened earlier in the day—but tagging along would help him solve that particular mystery.

And it would get him out of town. While he had zero enthusiasm for a road trip, it was better than the alternative—staying put and hiding from the press. 'I'm happy to take things slow, Bree,' he found himself saying.

A bad taste filled his mouth then. He had no right to invade her privacy or to spy on her or force a confidence she wasn't ready to share. 'Are you sure about this?' He searched her face. 'It's a really kind offer and one I don't deserve after what I said to you in the car on the way over here. I owe you an apology for that.'

She dismissed that with a wave of her hand. 'It's forgotten already. You were upset. Understandably so.'

Bree had always had a big heart. The three of them—he, Ryder and Blake—had teased her mercilessly when they'd been growing up. But whenever they'd been down, it had always been Bree that they'd turned to.

'I need to warn you there's going to be a lot of singing to ABBA. I have multiple playlists at the ready.'

That made him smile. Ever since the *Mamma Mia!* movies she'd been ABBA-mad. 'Can I negotiate for a little Creedence Clearwater Revival?'

It was one of their ongoing jokes and an oblique reference to the *Die Hard* franchise.

Mamma Mia! was all well and good, but it had nothing on *Die Hard 4*.

She laughed and for no reason at all some of the weight that pressed him flat lifted. 'I'm sure I can manage some Creedence, but no thrash metal.'

He was long past his thrash-metal days.

'Noah,' she said softly.

He glanced up.

'If you decide to come along, I want you to know you can jump ship at any time. You don't have to go all the way to Hobart.'

That was true. 'I could probably lose myself in Sydney for a few days. No one will be expecting to see me there.' It would give him a breather and mean he'd only be cramping Bree's style for part of her journey.

He hauled in a breath and nodded. 'Thanks, Bree. If you're sure I won't be cramping your style, then I'd like to accept your very kind offer and tag along.'

'Right, well…' She glanced at her brothers and then at him. 'All we need now is to pack you a suitcase.'

Damn it. He couldn't go back to his apartment. 'I'll have to buy something on the road.'

'Not necessary,' Ryder said. 'I grabbed the suitcase you'd packed for your honeymoon be-

fore that monster of a maid of honour tore off in
the bridal car.'

His honeymoon… He should be getting
ready—

'Also,' Bree said in her bossy tone, 'you don't
get to drive at all today.'

His head came up. 'I'm perfectly capable of
driving. I've been jilted, not crippled, and—'

She pointed at the beer he held. 'That's your
third and it's not even lunchtime yet.'

Damn! She was right. He couldn't remember
when he'd last had a beer this early in the day.
'Fine, whatever. What time did you want to set
off?' He did his best to keep the scowl out of
his voice.

She consulted her watch again. 'In an hour
and a half.'

Why couldn't they leave now? He wanted
away from this scene of defeat and humiliation
as fast as possible. He opened his mouth, but shut
it again when he recognised the stubborn light
in her eyes. She wouldn't budge.

'We're having lunch before we leave, and
you're putting something in your stomach besides beer, that's non-negotiable.'

He ground back a sigh. She was setting the
ground rules—going on as she meant to continue. She was the boss and he was merely a
passenger. He scowled at her. He couldn't help

it. But then his scowls had never had the slightest impact on her. He swung to Colin. 'Do you mind if I jump on your treadmill for half an hour?'

'Knock yourself out, son.'

He was barely out through the door, only partway down the hallway that led downstairs to Colin's home gym, before Bree's entire family jumped on her with varying bits of advice.

Folding his arms, he leaned against the wall and listened. It was probably beneath him to eavesdrop, but today he simply didn't have the strength to fight his baser instincts. Today he couldn't cope with any more surprises.

'You need to keep a close eye on him.'

'Don't let him get too morose.'

'And don't let him jump ship—at least not for the next two days.'

'I want daily updates.'

'And, darling, please make sure he eats something every day. We don't want him getting sick on top of everything else.'

This wasn't fair. All this pressure they were putting on her. He appreciated their support, but he couldn't ruin her holiday. She hadn't had a proper holiday in six or seven years, and while he might be throwing himself a big pity party, he had no right to drag Bree into the middle of that. She had big plans—they all knew that—and he'd be the lowest of the low if he inadvertently derailed them. He'd never forgive himself.

'But get him rolling drunk tonight. If he passes out he won't have to think about what happened today and—'

'Enough!' Bree's voice cut through the directives and general mayhem. 'I know what happened today was awful. I know it has to be a terrible blow for Noah. But he's a grown-up. And he's *not* an idiot. None of you have the right or any reason whatsoever to believe he'll do something stupid.'

Noah's head came up.

'I am not a nursemaid and I'm not going to order Noah around like he's a child. We're going to head south, put some distance between us and Brisbane's tabloid press, and sing loudly to whatever takes our fancy. We'll stop when we want to stop, and eat when we want to eat.'

Sounded like a brilliant plan to him.

'Also, I am *not* drinking beer and bourbon. But I'll sip a glass of Shiraz while Noah does *if* he decides he wants to drink beer and bourbon.'

Drinking beer and bourbon sounded like a hell of a good plan too.

'No more,' she said when everyone started talking at one another again.

Noah shot downstairs to the home gym before someone caught him listening. Bree had it all under control.

Blake and Ryder cornered him in the foyer after lunch where he was waiting for Bree so they could finally leave this mess of a day behind them.

'You sure you're okay with this plan, buddy?' Ryder asked. 'If you'd rather hunker down here at Mum and Dad's…?'

He shook his head. 'That would send me stir crazy and you know it. At least driving will give me the illusion of doing something.' And heading somewhere. Even if it was a lie and his life was stuck fast in a deep rut and he was spinning his wheels in the same spot.

Ryder grimaced.

Noah's gut clenched. 'What?' Was there more bad news?

'I know this isn't wholly within your power, but I'd appreciate it if you could keep Bree's name out of the papers for as long as the two of you travel together.'

'Hell, Ryder, it's not my plan that Bree be named in any fashion at all—before, after or in between.'

His friend raised his hands. 'I know. I know. Just thought I'd mention it.'

Hell, if the press linked them together… His gut churned. He could just imagine the salacious headlines. 'You have my word.'

'You know, mate…' Blake leaned against the wall '…it'd be great if you could get a heads-up on what this trip of Bree's is about. She's been as closed as a clam.'

Bree appeared at the end of the corridor, but her brothers had their backs to her and didn't see her. He met her eyes briefly, though he couldn't make out their expression. He recalled what she'd said about him earlier. Her words hadn't made him feel like a victim. They'd made him feel strong. 'In case you guys haven't noticed, Bree's a grown-up now. I'm not prying into her private business. If she wants you to know what she's up to, she'll tell you.'

When he met her gaze again, she was smiling.

CHAPTER TWO

THEY DIDN'T SAY much about anything until Bree had cleared the city and turned the car onto the highway heading south. She darted a glance across at Noah. He didn't have his eyes shut, wasn't pretending to be asleep in an attempt to avoid conversation. For the first time—or at least the first time in a long, long time—she noticed what a beautiful profile he had: square jaw, straight nose…firm, inviting lips.

'Eyes on the road, please, Bree,' he said without turning his head.

She reefed her gaze back to the front. He was right. She should give her full attention to the driving. Except a tiny part of her mind refused to obey her. If he wasn't pretending to be asleep… Did that mean he wanted to talk?

If he wanted to talk, she'd listen, sympathise, and cast all the aspersions he wanted on faithless Courtney's character. In short, she'd treat him like one of her girlfriends when they'd been dumped by some thoughtless, good-for-nothing louse.

She risked another quick glance at him. Except, for some reason, it was coming home to her now with a ferocity she couldn't ignore that Noah was about as opposite to one of her girlfriends as it was possible to get. He was a potent mix of half-bristling, half-slumbering masculinity.

It threw her because she'd never thought of him in that way before. Not really.

Her hands tightened about the steering wheel. And she wasn't going to start thinking about him in that way now either! Lord, talk about asking for an avalanche of trouble to land on your head.

She forced her hands to unclench. She was a woman. She could see the guy was hot. But even if she actually found herself truly attracted to Noah there was no way on God's green earth that she'd ever get involved with a guy on the rebound. Especially at this point in her life. She was about to turn her entire world on its head. She didn't have the time for a man—*any* man.

But in the coming year she was going to need her family *and* her friends. And as Noah was practically family *and* one of her very best friends…

A tremble shivered through the very centre of her. Was she really going to do this? *Could* she do it? What about The Plan? If she went through with this she'd be smashing it to smithereens, and The Plan had been her safety net for the last seven years.

Gah, don't think about it now!

She gnawed on her bottom lip. She'd have time enough to go through it all once she'd left Noah behind in Sydney. She had days and days yet on the road to sort through it all. She and Tina would work it all out.

For the moment she needed to focus on Noah.

Blowing out a long breath, she kept her gaze trained ahead. She could at least ask the question. 'Did you want to talk?'

She wouldn't push. Pushing him would bring him to full-bristling masculine life and she had a feeling she should be doing all she could to lull the beast into full slumber.

'Not unless it's about why you're heading to Tassie.'

She recalled his words to her brothers—*'It's Bree's private business...she's a grown-up.'* Those words had wrapped her in a golden glow, warming her to the soles of her feet. But even as her lips curved upwards, she shook her head. 'Like I keep telling everyone, I haven't had a holiday in over six years.'

She wasn't ready to talk about the real reason.

'If you want to see Tasmania it'd be quicker to fly and hire a car once you got there.'

'Ah, but it's not about the destination. It's about the journey.'

He gave a low laugh that had all the fine hairs on her arms lifting in a delicious little shiver. 'Fine, keep your secrets and your inspirational platitudes to yourself for the time being, Busy Bree.'

It was the nickname he'd given her when she was eight. She hadn't heard him use it in *forever*.

'But be warned, I'll ask again.'

'Naturally. You're as nosy as Blake and Ryder.'

Eventually she'd have to tell everyone. But she wasn't ready to do that just yet. As soon as she said the words it would make them real.

'They love you, Bree. They worry. It's natural. It comes with the territory of being the youngest.'

'Perhaps, but, as you pointed out to them, I'm all grown up now.'

'But—'

'And their constant vigilance—which you call concern—makes me feel like a screw-up.' It reminded her of how badly she'd messed up in the past. Maybe she was being paranoid, but she now felt as if they were constantly keeping tabs on her.

'Nobody thinks you're a screw-up.'

It made her think they were simply waiting for her to mess up again.

He turned in his seat to face her more fully, but

she refused to send him so much as the briefest of glances. It took a concerted effort to ease her foot off the accelerator and not speed.

'Bree, *nobody* thinks you're a screw-up. Everyone, your entire family, is proud of you. We're all proud of how hard you've been working and all you've achieved.'

'It doesn't change the fact that their constant vigilance, their constant worry, makes me *feel* like a screw-up.'

From the corner of her eye she saw him open his mouth, but he shut it again and settled back in his seat. 'Fair enough,' he finally said.

Unlike her brothers, Noah had always heard what she said—he acknowledged her feelings without the need to impress his own version of the truth on her. She'd always loved that about him. 'Thank you,' she murmured softly.

'Do *you* think you're a screw-up?'

She bit her lip. 'No.'

But she knew he'd heard her hesitation. While she'd had The Plan—and had stuck to it—she'd been confident all would be well. But now she was turning The Plan on its head, she felt rudderless.

She swallowed and ignored the panicked pounding of her pulse. All she had to do was come up with a new plan, that was all. She was on holiday…lots of wide, open spaces and long

stretches of road…plenty of time to work on
Plan B.

That was the real reason she'd opted to drive
to Hobart rather than fly—the open road, the
wind in her hair, and all the time in the world
to consider her options and find a way to make
it all…work. It had seemed the perfect strategy.

Except now she had a giant-sized distraction
in the shape of Noah.

But it was only a temporary one. They'd stay
at Coffs Harbour tonight and would be in Sydney tomorrow afternoon. With Noah remaining
behind in Sydney, there'd still be oodles of time
to think and plan…to come to terms with her
new future.

'Music?' she asked, because she didn't want
to pursue this conversation any further.

He heaved a mock sigh. 'Fine. Hit me with
ABBA.'

Grinning, she hit play on her carefully curated
playlist, created after lunch to remove all slow,
sad and lovelorn ballads as well as any songs
that mentioned 'I do' or weddings in any fashion whatsoever.

He laughed when he discovered she'd alter-
nated ABBA with Creedence Clearwater Revival. For the next hour they both belted out the
lyrics to the songs, woefully torturing the high
notes and taking alternate parts in the duets. On

the surface they were having more fun than it had seemed possible earlier in the day, but all the while she was aware of the storm simmering inside the man beside her.

When a song came to an end, he checked his watch. 'I'd like to listen to the news.'

She wanted to talk him out of it, but one glance at his face and she turned off the music and gestured to the console for him to choose whichever radio station he wanted.

The cancelled wedding made the breaking headlines: *Shock Halt to Society Wedding!* The full story claimed that Courtney Fraser had called a shock halt to the wedding just after the service had started, with neither bride nor groom reappearing after a short conference and neither available for comment now. 'Sources close to the couple quote irreconcilable differences as the reason the wedding did not go ahead as planned. The father of the bride says he supports his daughter's decision. It's believed the bride has fled to the family's private island retreat in the Mediterranean while the groom is holed up at his friend and business partner Ryder Allenby's inner-city condominium.'

With a savage stab of his finger, Noah turned the radio back off.

'I'm sorry,' she said quietly.

'They made me sound pathetic.'

'No, they didn't!'

'I should've given a statement.'

'And come across as angry instead? That would've been ten times worse and you know it. They'd have made it sound like she was in her right mind to cancel the wedding. Or,' she added when he opened his mouth, 'you'd have looked and sounded so utterly shell-shocked, as if the rug had been literally pulled out from under you. And while that's absolutely natural and an understandable reaction, the press would've had a feeding frenzy with it. You'd have been portrayed as a hapless victim, which *would've* been pathetic, while Courtney would've been made out as the villain of the piece.'

'She is the villain of the piece!'

She swallowed. 'I'm still glad you didn't feed her to the wolves.'

With a muttered oath he dragged a hand down his face. 'I just hate feeling like I ran away.'

'You didn't run away.'

'That's what it *feels* like,' he shot back, raising an eyebrow full of pregnant meaning.

He was right. He'd treated her feelings with respect. She should show him the same courtesy. She nodded. 'I'm sorry you feel that way. I know you're not a coward. And you can make a statement whenever you damn well please, but the simple fact is you owe the press nothing.'

'Where's that line, though? Ryder and I are more than happy to exploit the press when we want the publicity for Fitness Ark.'

Fitness Ark was the name of their highly successful gym franchise and the name of the brand of fitness machines Noah had patented.

'You and Ryder didn't sign a contract to bare your souls in exchange for said publicity. What would you expect from Ryder in the same situation?'

He was quiet for so long she'd started to think she'd come up with an argument that had finally held some weight with him.

'Ryder would never find himself in that situation,' he said quietly. 'He's too smart for that.'

'Rubbish!'

He stiffened at her rudeness but she didn't care.

She glared. 'I hope you were touching wood when you said that. That's exactly the kind of challenge one should never put out in the universe.'

'Why the hell didn't you think me and Courtney well suited?' he flung at her.

She wondered how long he'd been holding the question back. She'd been expecting an outburst since they'd left Brisbane, but the shock of it now still made her heart hammer in her chest. She had to tread carefully. There were so many reasons but to detail them all would be like kicking a man when he was down.

Why on earth had he wanted to marry a woman he didn't love anyhow? She sent him a sidelong glance. Short answer—maybe he'd thought himself in love with her.

'I want an answer, Bree.'

'Even if it hurts your feelings or you find my answer confronting?'

'Even then,' he bit out.

'You know this is just my opinion, right? There's every chance I'm wrong?'

'Absolutely.'

He wholly and totally believed she'd be wrong. She thrust her jaw out. She *wasn't* wrong. 'Courtney tried to change you.'

He swung to face her, his knee banging against the centre console. *'What?'*

To her right a sugar-cane crop stretched for as far as the eye could see. To her left the blue sliver of a river snaking through the landscape glinted and flashed. She let the serenity of the landscape filter into her soul before opening her mouth again. 'It seems to me that if people are well suited then they accept each other as they are and don't try to change each other. You didn't try to change her.'

'She was perfect the way she was.'

Bree snorted. 'So not true. She just wants

everyone to think she is.' Which meant calling off this morning's wedding had to have taken a lot of courage, because appearances mattered something fierce to Courtney.

'She's not exactly what I'd call warm and pally either.' She'd never once made Bree feel welcome at any of her soirées or made any real gesture of friendship.

'You just have to get to know her better.'

She didn't want to know Courtney better. They had zero in common. 'Before you met Courtney, what did you like to do?' She didn't wait for him to answer. 'You used to like hiking and camping, jet skiing and water sports, playing indoor cricket and hockey. You'd try a new sport—rock climbing or white-water rafting—just for fun. When was the last time you did any of that?'

'I needed to make time for Courtney.'

'You didn't have to give *all* of it up.'

'That was my decisions, not hers.'

'You sure about that?'

'Of course I am.'

'She manipulated you,' Bree continued. 'Instead of doing any of the things you wanted to do, you did all the things she wanted to do— the theatre appreciation society, the wine club… society dinners. On and on and on until you no longer had time for even your weekly one-hour indoor cricket game on a Wednesday night.'

And even then Courtney hadn't been happy. Noah deserved so much better.

Noah blinked as the truth of Bree's words burrowed into the hard grey matter of his brain and stuck there with barbs that refused to let go.

'I enjoyed doing those things with Courtney.' But had he?

Or had he simply told himself that he *should* enjoy them?

His jaw started to ache. The right kind of man, the kind of man who could win a woman like Courtney—the kind of man he wanted to be—would appreciate wine societies and foreign film clubs and mixing with Brisbane's elite.

In his heart of hearts, though, he still preferred a game of indoor cricket.

Which just went to prove what a failure he was. His bride had seen through his façade. She'd seen beneath the money and success to the rough and ready kid from the wrong side of the tracks—and it had appalled her so much she'd fled. *On their wedding day.*

His hands clenched. Courtney Fraser had been his ideal, the perfect woman, and everything he aspired to be worthy of. She was polished, sophisticated…charming, and she came from a good family—all the things he wasn't and didn't.

She knew about art history, how to host a dinner party for a foreign diplomat and who to be seen with, along with a corresponding knowledge of who to avoid. For God's sake, she knew when to use who or whom in a sentence!

What did he know? He knew how to engineer fitness machines; he knew how to calibrate them to create the perfect workout experience for every single level from raw beginner to advanced athlete. He knew how to broker business partnerships and drive a hard bargain. And he knew how to duck a punch. He sure as hell didn't know how to grease the wheels of social intercourse, and his grammar was second-rate at best.

Being married to Courtney would've given him access to the things he lacked. She'd completed him. As he said—his ideal.

Except his perfect woman *didn't* jilt him at the altar. A scowl built through him. Obviously he hadn't completed her. She didn't need a guy from the wrong side of the tracks made good. Seriously, what did a guy like him have to bring to the table to tempt a woman like her?

Money? said a cynical voice in his head.

He shook that thought off. Courtney's family came from old money. She'd joined her father's law firm as a divorce lawyer and would make partner by the time she was thirty-five. Courtney Fraser was beautiful, driven, ambitious, and too damn intelligent to hitch her wagon to a guy like him. And who could blame her?

She'd always been out of his league. He'd just been a fool for not realising sooner.

'Out of your league?'

Bree snorted, and he realised he'd spoken those last words out loud.

'What a load of superannuated, noxious old garbage with prawn shells that have been sitting out in the burning sun for over a week!' Bree's nose wrinkled and then she rolled her eyes. 'I take it we're up to the pity-party phase of proceedings?'

He had to bite back what felt like an entirely inappropriate grin. Bree could never just say *garbage*. She had to add a ton of qualifiers so the listener wouldn't mistake her meaning. To an outsider she'd sound unsympathetic, insensitive, but he knew her too well. She'd do everything she could to prevent him from descending into a cycle of despondency and shame...to stop him from wallowing in today's humiliation.

He sobered. Except the events of the day were more than just an average case of the blues or a minor setback. This kicked a guy's legs out from under him, gutted him, and left him bleeding and scarred for life.

'You were plenty good enough for Princess

Courtney, but the only person who couldn't see it was you.'

'You never liked her, so excuse me if I consider your comments a little biased.'

'I didn't know her well enough to either like or dislike her.'

But when she glanced at him, he raised an eyebrow and she reefed her gaze back to the road again and blew out a breath.

'Okay, I was leaning more on the side of dislike,' she muttered. 'I'll admit that much. But I hadn't given up hope that I was wrong about her and that at some indeterminate time in the future we'd become friends.'

'Why the dislike?' A lot of women didn't like Courtney, but he'd noticed that those same women also felt intimidated by her achievements, her intelligence and her effortless polish. He'd have not placed Bree among their number, though, and the thought started a low burn in his gut.

As if she could read his thoughts, and she probably could, she said, 'I can forgive her for her model-style figure, that perfect face and a complexion to die for. I can even forgive her the university medal she won for academic excellence, not to mention the Premier's Award for her charity work.'

Something inside him started to lighten. He

should've known better. Bree wasn't the kind of woman to feel jealous of other women. 'What couldn't you forgive?'

She was quiet for several long moments. 'She stopped you from coming to Sunday night dinners.'

Sunday night dinner was an Allenby family tradition, started back before he knew them. Of course now, with all the kids grown up, absences were common. But whenever possible the entire family would gather at Janice and Colin's for a roast dinner and family catch-up. He'd had a longstanding invitation from the age of eleven onwards.

'That was my doing, not hers.' His mind started to race. But was it? 'Besides, I didn't stop coming. I just didn't make it quite so often.'

'You went four months without showing your face on a Sunday night. Mum missed you.'

A bad taste filled his mouth. How could he have been so insensitive? 'My fault,' he repeated.

'Courtney had a standing invitation. Everyone made sure she knew she was welcome. But how often did she come?'

He could count them all on the fingers of one hand. She'd only accompanied him to the Allenbys' four times, and the last had to have been over seven months ago. He'd thought each evening had gone well, everyone had got along just fine and there'd been lots of laughter. Courtney had told him on each occasion that she'd really enjoyed herself, and yet…in two years she'd only accompanied him four times.

Why the hell hadn't that fact bothered him more before today?

Because yesterday he'd been too busy seeing her as perfect?

He dragged a hand down his face, starting to see the flimsiness of the excuses he'd made on her behalf in his own mind. They'd been easy to make, though. After all, she was a busy woman with a lot of demands on her time. Her excuses whenever he'd extended the family night invitation had seemed genuinely plausible…understandable.

But actions spoke louder than words. She'd known how much the Allenbys meant to him and yet she still hadn't found the time, not once in seven months, to join him there for another family dinner.

'So there you have it, Noah.' She flexed her hands on the wheel. 'That's why I didn't like her. I felt she was stealing you away—that we were losing you rather than gaining her. She was always perfectly polite and pleasant, but it was clear she didn't want…'

'Didn't want?'

Bree lifted one shoulder. 'Didn't want to be

part of us.' She continued to stare doggedly out of the window at the road ahead, and he found himself aching for her to turn and look at him, however briefly. 'Which is fair enough, I suppose.'

No, it damn well wasn't! He'd given Courtney everything she'd asked for. Why couldn't she have done this one thing for him?

For the first time since he and Courtney had started dating, he saw a significant crack in their relationship and it made him suck in a breath. If he had married her, would she have forced him to choose between her and the Allenbys? The thought sent icy fingers creeping across his skull.

'She played on your insecurities too, and I found that hard to forgive.'

He stiffened, and then immediately made himself relax and laugh. 'Insecurities? What insecurities?'

She threw her head back and laughed—a deep warm sound so full of genuine humour and affection that he blinked. It should've jarred his nerves. Instead a strange warmth stirred in his blood. 'You, Blake and Ryder are all so alike. It's hilarious! Me, macho and indestructible.' She beat on her chest Tarzan fashion.

She laughed again and he started, realising he'd been staring at her chest, his gaze drawn there when she beat on it. He gulped. When had Bree developed curves like that?

'Everyone has insecurities, tough guy.'

He dragged his gaze away, forced himself to focus on her words rather than the pounding of his pulse.

Did Bree have insecurities? He'd never really thought about it. She always seemed so together and driven—knew what she wanted and how to go about getting it. 'Fine, Ms Sigmund Freud, what are my insecurities?'

She glanced at him, eyes wide as if his question had startled her, but the expression in them gentled. 'Oh, Noah.'

Something in her tone made him swallow. Her knuckles whitened about the steering wheel and he wanted to call the question back but he couldn't. Because he was macho and a tough guy and he didn't want to lose face. He'd lost enough face for one day. 'Well?'

'You said it yourself—you never felt worthy of Courtney. You always felt she was out of your league.'

His every muscle tensed and cramped.

'You don't know how wrong you are. Though I know you won't believe me, you're worth a hundred Courtneys.' Her knuckles turned white again. 'Courtney knew you felt that way too— knew your background bugged you.'

He folded his arms to hide the way his insides shrivelled at her words. 'Courtney finally realised I wouldn't fit into her perfectly polished world. And with that came the realisation she couldn't go through with the wedding. Damn pity she didn't come to that conclusion prior to the wedding ceremony with two hundred guests in attendance, though.'

Bree glanced at him. 'You're wrong, you know? She never considered you not worthy or herself somehow above you. I might not have liked her very much but I'll give credit where it's due. She led a privileged life, but I don't think she was a snob.'

'Like you said, you didn't know her.' He knew he was being unfair, but who would blame him after what Courtney had done today?

'I'm not a trophy you get to hold aloft,' Bree said quietly.

He shifted, the car seat suddenly hard beneath his backside. 'I never thought of her as a trophy.' *He hadn't.* But a sense of unease wormed into the centre of his soul all the same.

'She obviously thought you did.'

She glanced at him as if expecting him to say something, but he had nothing to say. He'd given Courtney everything. He'd given her his full attention, his total support…not to mention his time. Whatever she'd wanted to do, he'd always been on board with. He'd given her free rein with the wedding, and had left the choice of where they'd live once their married life had started up to her. It still hadn't been enough. *He* hadn't been enough.

He wanted to say good riddance and be done with her. He wanted to feel as if he'd dodged a bullet. But all he felt was small and cheap—the way his parents had made him feel as a child. The way he'd been fighting against for thirty years. He wanted to crawl into some dark hidden hole, the way he'd used to crawl under the house as a little kid to avoid his father's abuse and his mother's backhands.

He'd worked hard over the past ten years—had achieved more than he'd ever dreamed possible. And yet here he was feeling like crap again, despite all of that. This was what happened when you gave someone that kind of power over you.

Well, no more. Never again. He hadn't had any choice as a child, but he had the choice now as a grown man.

'Let's have some music,' Bree finally said.

Inane pop immediately filled the car and while Bree hummed along, he couldn't join in. He knew her casual attitude was simply a show of bravado, the glances she sent him when she didn't think he was looking confirmed it, but he didn't have the energy to ease her mind. The events of the day had finally caught up with him, and he was starting to see the impossibility of the dreams he'd once dared to dream. What an idiot he'd been.

He stared out of the window, not seeing the rich farmland, green after recent rains, or the signposts for popular beachside holiday destinations—Yamba, Caloundra, Byron Bay—all of it darkened by the grimness of his thoughts.

Family life, a wife and kids, were not meant for the likes of him. A howl started up at the centre of him, but he resolutely ignored it. He was a ridiculously successful businessman, the Allenbys were his surrogate family, and he had a circle of friends he'd die for. It was enough. He refused to want more.

If Courtney had given him an ultimatum, had asked him outright to choose between her and the Allenbys, he'd have sent her packing. There were no two ways about it. But she hadn't—not in so many words. Now that he started to see what Bree had seen, though, the scales were falling from his eyes.

Courtney's tactics had been far less direct, but more insidious for all of that. How long would it have taken him to work it out on his own— her weaning him away from them inch by careful inch? Once he'd worked it out, he'd have not stood for it. And if Courtney hadn't given way it would've driven a wedge between them.

Was that why she'd called a halt to the wedding? Had she realised she'd never be able to wholly steal him away from the Allenbys? Why the hell would she want to anyway?

Things inside him went hard and cold. Courtney had wanted to make him over, mould him, into something more appropriate. And he'd wanted her to! He'd yearned for the polish and sophistication, the ease and composure, to navigate a world so far removed from the one that he'd grown up in.

Only he hadn't seen where it might lead— the less than favourable consequences associated with such an overhaul.

Like he'd said, *What an idiot.*

They reached Coffs Harbour just before seven o'clock. He laughed at the spartan motel rooms Bree had booked. 'I see you're going all out here, Bree, and really treating yourself.'

'Coffs Harbour was always just a layover. As I'm going to be spending two or three nights in Sydney, I'm planning to stay somewhere nicer there. This…' she gestured around '…was just a convenient place to get some shut-eye. So…did you want to do anything? I was just going to grab takeaway unless you want to eat out.'

'God, no.'

She nodded as if she'd figured that was what he'd say. 'What would you like?'

'Beer and bourbon.' He fished out his wallet and held his credit card towards her. 'And grab a bottle of Shiraz for yourself.'

She ignored the card. 'How about a side order of pizza to go with that?'

'Whatever you want.' He wasn't the slightest bit hungry.

With that, she left and it was only once he was alone that Noah realised how grounding Bree's presence had been all day.

He'd been left at the altar. His bride had jilted him. The life he'd mapped out—the life he'd hungered for with every atom inside him—was gone.

He'd failed.

He was a failure.

He paced the room. 'C'mon, Bree, hurry up.' He wanted to get good and drunk before his thoughts ate him alive.

CHAPTER THREE

'DON'T LET THE pizza go cold.' Bree swiped the can of beer Noah had grabbed from the little bar fridge in her room and set it back inside before pushing the pizza box into his arms instead. 'Have one slice at least. Please?'

She planted herself in front of the fridge and folded her arms. Noah had already drunk two beers in quick succession, and while she knew that he and her brothers could drink a lot when they put their minds to it, that didn't mean they'd not wake up with sore heads the next day.

She didn't kid herself—Noah was going to have a hangover tomorrow, probably one of mammoth proportions. She wasn't even going to try and stop him from drowning his sorrows. But she'd do all she could to mitigate the damage.

He could pick her up and set her aside easily enough, and grab what was left of the six-pack. She fancied she saw that notion momentarily flash through his mind, but he eventually just shrugged and flashed her a grin. *That* grin. The grin she'd seen fell more women over the years than she could count.

'I'll have two pieces if it'll make you feel better, Breanna.'

Dear God. The way he said her name in that lazy, husky-as-sin voice, enunciating each syllable as if her name were a delectable dish worth savouring. It made her aware that they were alone together in a hotel room. Her heart pitter-pattered to a faster beat while warmth gathered beneath her breastbone and rose to flood her cheeks.

Ooh, no, no, no. She wasn't going to have those kinds of thoughts about Noah. She wasn't going to become one of Noah's Nymphettes.

Noah's Nymphettes and the Twinses' Minxes were what she'd dubbed the multitude of girls that had hovered in the three boys' orbits from the time they'd hit puberty.

And once Bree had reached puberty, Bree's Bad Boys had been added to the mix.

The last thought came out of nowhere, making her flinch.

'Hell, Bree, I'll stop drinking altogether if it bugs you that much.'

He'd taken the pizza box across to the bed and settled on one side with the pillows at his back, and while he looked relaxed and at ease she sensed the keenness behind the warm hazel of his eyes. She realised then that he'd thought *he'd* made her flinch.

She shook her head. 'I don't mind you drinking, Noah, but I am going to make you eat something first.'

She dropped a bag of salt and vinegar crisps to the bed—his favourite—along with a couple of bars of fruit and nut chocolate—her favourite—before settling on the other side of the bed and helping herself to a piece of pizza. 'And a little later on I'm going to make you drink big glasses of water and you're going to promise to drink them.'

'Cross my heart.' He pressed a hand to his chest before reaching for another slice of pizza. 'No pineapple?'

She was pro pineapple on pizza. He wasn't. 'I wasn't giving you any reason to refuse to eat it.'

He was quiet for several long seconds and just stared at her. 'You're a hell of a friend, you know that?'

'Absolutely.' She turned the compliment off lightly, but it warmed her to the soles of her feet.

'Today's been a bitch of a day, but—'

The golden highlights in his hazel eyes caught the light, making them spark. His eyes looked as deep and soulful as a galaxy. Her breath stuttered. 'But?' she choked out.

'But that hasn't stopped me from enjoying hanging out with you.'

Slowly she nodded. 'I know what you mean. It's the weirdest thing, right?' It should've been an unrelentingly bad day.

Not that it hadn't been bad. The morning had been appalling…atrocious…gob-smackingly awful. But there'd been pockets of time during the drive when things had been…*nice*. It seemed an insipid word to use, but that didn't make it any less appropriate. Parts of today, hanging out with Noah, had been nice.

Obviously neither of them had expected that. Perhaps it was testament to the resilience of the human spirit? Or simply the comfort that could be found in old friends? Whatever, she was grateful for it.

She reached for the remote. 'There has to be a game on. If memory serves me correct the women's soccer team play an international friendly tonight and—'

'I think I should feel more gutted than I am.'

Whoa!

She tossed the remote to the bedside table with a clatter and swung back to him. He'd leapt up to grab another beer. She shook her head when he gestured at the bottle of wine she'd bought. She'd only bought it to look sociable. She had no intention of drinking it. At least, not tonight.

Instinct told her to stay alert. Not to dull them…not to let her guard down and let the wildness inside her win. It had been trying to break free ever since she'd agreed to Tina's plan, but she *would* keep a rein on it. Besides, tonight was for Noah. She needed to keep her wits sharp and do all she could to be the friend he needed.

'You've had your heart broken, Bree.' The bed dipped as he settled back down beside her. 'Is this normal?'

Nobody in her circle ever mentioned Otis or the heartbreak she'd suffered at his hands, not even obliquely.

He shrugged. 'I know nobody talks about it, and I hope you don't mind, but…'

'I don't mind,' she said slowly. She knew everyone only avoided the topic out of respect for her, for fear of upsetting her. At the time she'd just wanted to bury the experience and forget it had ever happened. She wondered now if that had been the best strategy.

She glanced at Noah. 'You looked pretty gutted to me earlier.'

He grimaced.

'I don't know if heartbreak is the same for everyone, but in my experience the grief comes in waves. One moment you're feeling down and out as if nothing good or bright can ever happen again, and then something dumb will catch your attention and take you out of yourself for a bit.'

'Dumb…like what?'

'The football scores might flash up on the telly and you'll see your team has had a huge win in a derby match and you'll jump out of your chair and do a victory dance. Or a catchy tune comes on the radio and without noticing you'll find yourself singing along. Or you hear a funny story and find yourself laughing out loud.'

She met his gaze and shrugged. 'So in the midst of the awfulness you have these moments where you forget the awfulness and feel…almost normal, almost happy. I found it a bit confronting at first.'

Her eyes burned as she remembered how she'd let down everyone she'd loved. She'd let them down so badly. She still hated that. It was why she was so worried about throwing out The Plan now.

In changing the direction her life was about to take… Dear God, what guarantee did she have that she wouldn't fail again? She couldn't afford to fail. Not at this. Not when so many people were relying on her. She had to find a way to make sure she wouldn't go off the rails again, to stay on track.

'Bree?'

She shook herself, forced her mind back to the

present conversation, sent Noah what she hoped was a smile. 'When the Otis situation exploded, it felt as if my whole world had been turned upside down.'

His hand closed around hers. 'I know.'

The pain in his eyes made her suck in a breath. That pain... Her heart started to pound. Had she read the situation between him and Courtney wrong? Had he truly loved the other woman and she'd just been too blind to see it?

She swallowed and forced herself to answer his question as fully and frankly as she could. 'So it felt wrong, disorienting, to find that I still enjoyed some of the things I had prior to the heartbreak.'

If Noah truly did love Courtney, then she had to help him fix things.

'Waves,' he mused. 'That sounds like a good way to describe it.'

'It happens the other way too. You'll be happily going along feeling fine—thinking you're doing fine—when a memory slams into you out of nowhere and hurtles you back into a black pit of depression.'

'What kind of memories?'

That old heaviness settled over her. 'Odd things—like the foot massage he gave you after the particularly awful day you'd had and how good it felt—not just the massage but the fact he understood how bad your day had been and wanted to make it better. Or the time you went to the cinema to see a horror film together and he held your hand all the way through it, even though he was also juggling popcorn and a drink, and he let you hide your face in his shoulder… and never ever teased you about it, not once, because you begged him not to. Or the night you went out on the town and it was freezing on the way home and he put his jacket around your shoulders and it was warm and it smelled like him…' she'd always loved Otis's scent '…and it was a still night and the stars were all out and then he kissed you and told you he loved you and you thought there would never be a more perfect moment in your entire life.'

They were the memories she'd tried to forget. Some things, though, refused to be forgotten. The memory of what it was like to feel loved and wanted, for one…or how—

Noah swore and she crashed back into the present with a thump.

He seized another beer, and she realised he'd finished the previous one in record time. She opened the crisps and held them out to him. 'Salt and vinegar,' she said somewhat unnecessarily.

He took a handful, scowling at her. 'And has there?'

'Has there what?'

'Has there ever been a more perfect moment in your life, Bree?'

He enunciated every syllable with a savage accuracy that made her throat ache. What memory had she just resurrected for him that was burned into his brain for all eternity? She wanted to tell him she was sorry for bringing it to roaring life, except she knew he'd scorn her apology.

'I take it that's a no, then?'

He lifted the beer and drank it down too hard and fast. She bit into a crisp with a savage crunch. 'I have high expectations that it'll be eclipsed in the future.'

He lowered the beer to stare at her. She shrugged at him. 'The thing about broken hearts, Noah, is that they do eventually mend.'

'Your heart isn't broken any more?'

Why on earth was she wasting calories on crisps? She reached for a chocolate bar. 'It's not broken any more. I'm glad I'm no longer with Otis.'

She hadn't spoken about any of this in any detail with anyone, but now that she'd started she couldn't seem to stop. 'For a long time I bounced. One day I was ready to forgive Otis for every wrong he'd ever done me, making every excuse for him that I could—and, believe me, there was no excuse too small. I ached for things to go back the way they were before everything exploded.

I'd make deals with the universe—if the universe gave him back to me, I'd make sure he never took drugs again.'

Noah groaned and rubbed a hand over his face.

She nodded. 'I know. It was sobering to realise there were days when I didn't have an ounce of pride. But then there were other days when I'd be burning with anger and outrage at what he'd done to me, how much he'd betrayed me, and I'd swear that nothing would ever prevail upon me to take him back. Eventually I started having more of those days than I did the others.' Thank God.

She pointed the bar of fruit and nut at him. 'One of the good things, once you've gained a little distance, is you remember all the annoying things about them and you start to see all the reasons you weren't suited.'

Narrowed eyes raked her face. 'Like what?'

She could practically see the thought in his mind—it was like a flashing neon sign above his head—*Courtney is perfect*. No, she darn well wasn't!

She bit into her chocolate bar, letting the sweetness coat her tongue. 'Not having to put up with his sulking fits when he didn't get his own way—he could brood over something for days. I didn't like his taste in comedians either. I like smart, good-natured comedy, not smut or mean humour. So now I never have to watch another comedy show like that for as long as I live.'

She crunched another crisp because the crunch was too satisfying. 'Oh!' She tapped her head as if she'd forgotten something important. 'There's the small fact that the entire the time we were together he was doing drugs. So, yeah, there's that.'

'Bree—'

'Now it's your turn.'

'What? I—'

'Three things that annoyed you about Courtney.'

'There's nothing—'

'How long did it take her to get ready for a night out?' She had two brothers. She was well versed in the peccadillos of the female population.

He straightened. 'It'd take her two hours minimum! What the hell is that all about? And she'd never leave the house without a full face of makeup—even if she was only going to the gym.' He shook his head as if the vagaries of womankind made no sense at all.

'I bet she really appreciated it when you belched too.'

That made him snort. 'I learned early on to leave the room if I was going to belch. God forbid I do anything so uncouth in her presence. Which, of course, means a guy can never relax for a minute whenever she's around, not even in his own house.'

'Well, there you go. You can now belch to your heart's content.'

'And I'll never have to watch another one of those dark, bleak foreign films she's so crazy about. Or feel guilty for watching a footy game on TV rather than doing something to improve my mind.'

Indignation swelled in her chest. 'She wanted you to improve your mind?'

He spread his hands. 'I know.'

Bree started to giggle. 'I hope you told her one couldn't improve upon perfection.'

His mouth dropped open to form a perfect O and then he threw his head back with a roar of laughter, and the shaking of the bed made Bree laugh harder until they were both laughing so hard it almost hurt.

The release in the tension that had bound them up tight all day was welcome, but left her feeling spent when it had finally subsided.

Noah swore and reached for the bottle of bourbon. 'I thought I was going to get it all, Bree. I thought I was going to live the life I'd always dreamed. I thought Courtney was my perfect woman—the ying to my yang. You know the spiel—*You complete me...yada-yada-yada.*'

Her heart clenched at the bitterness lacing his words.

He took a long pull on the bottle, not even bothering with a glass. 'I didn't expect life to always be rosy and perfect, because nobody's ever is. But I still thought we'd achieve the really important things—children, family, supporting each other, making a difference in the community. Children,' he repeated on a harsh laugh. 'Hell, I thought we'd grow old together!'

The rawness in his voice, the bleakness in his eyes, made hers burn.

'I don't know how the hell I'm supposed to go forward from here.'

She reached across and gripped his hand. 'You don't have to work that out all at once. You sure as hell don't have to work it out tonight. And you don't work it out on your own. You take it one day at a time. And what you do is you rely on your friends, because we'll all help you through it. And you will get through it, Noah, because you're strong and you're smart.'

He stared at her, and just for a moment it looked as if he'd stopped drowning—as if her words had provided him with a lifeline. But then he glanced away and she knew it was only a front. 'I know it's not the same, Noah, but we're all here for you—we're all in your corner.'

He was quiet for a moment, but then he nodded. 'It does help, Bree, knowing you guys have my back. It helps a lot.'

But his heart had been broken. And she knew from experience how long and hard the journey back from that took. How could she have misjudged his feelings for Courtney so badly? 'Noah—'

'No more, Bree, let's just watch the game.'

He took another swig from his bottle and she knew it would be for the best to let the subject drop for now. She grabbed him a big glass of water and insisted he drink it before turning on the TV to watch the replay of the women's soccer match.

Noah finally flaked out a bit after two a.m. On her bed. She'd chosen her room as the 'let's hang out in here' room, as she'd thought it might keep Noah in check more…that he'd simply leave when he'd had enough and wanted to be morose on his own.

She tucked his room key into her back pocket. Fine, she'd take his room instead. 'You're going to have a hell of a head when you wake up, Noah Fitzgerald,' she said, pulling off his shoes. He was lying on top of the covers so she covered him with the throw rug from the foot of the bed and placed a glass of water on the bedside table, making sure the pathway to the bathroom was clear. She left the lamp beside the door on, but dimmed it low.

She glanced down at his sleeping form, her gut clenching tight. Courtney had broken his heart. And now his dreams were dust.

Her hands fisted. She'd been so certain he wasn't in love with the other woman. She'd been so sure he'd been in love with an ideal rather than the reality. But what the hell did she know? She'd been in love with a drug dealer who, when busted, had told the police he'd been working for her. She knew nothing!

On impulse, she smoothed the dark hair from his brow and bent down to press a kiss to his forehead. 'Goodnight, Noah.'

When she eased away, dark smoky eyes flecked with gold stared into hers as if plumbing the depths of her soul. For a moment it hadn't been Noah's eyes she'd stared into but a stranger's. A beguiling stranger that made her blood heat and had the wind roaring in her ears.

Noah had never looked at her like that before.

With a mouth that had gone strangely dry, she stumbled backwards. 'Sleep tight,' she managed in a strangled tone before turning and fleeing the room.

Noah cracked one eye open at the sound of the door to his room opening. He winced when one of the curtains at the front window was partially pushed to one side to let in some light. He winced even though the light didn't strike any part of his face, as if the opener of the curtain had been careful to shield him from the ill effects of blinding sunlight on oversensitive eyes.

His temples pounded, and his mouth tasted of a rank mixture of bourbon and salt and vinegar crisps. He ran his tongue around disgustingly furry teeth as his stomach burned acid. He remained *very* still to counter the nausea circling at the edges of everything, waiting to claim him.

How much had he drunk last night? He didn't dare reach out to pat the floor and find the bourbon bottle to check how much was left, in case it overset his current steadyish equilibrium.

A zip opened and closed—a suitcase, he guessed—and then a rustling as someone moved towards the bed. A hand came into view as it placed a package on the bedside table.

'Bree?' he croaked, and then wished he hadn't as an electrical storm started flashing and thundering through his head.

'You're awake?'

She kept her voice low and if he could've moved without throwing up, he'd have hugged her. 'Not for long if I have any say in the matter,' he muttered.

'If it's any consolation, you can stay there all day. I've booked us in for another night.'

He stiffened. *Damn.* Her road trip!

He groaned. *Don't move.*

'We've switched rooms too, by the way. Your suitcase is just inside the door.'

He'd flaked out in her room? On her bed? Bad form. Really bad form.

'There are headache tablets and water on the bedside table if you want either.'

She was a saint. 'Thank you.'

He wanted to tell her she was a man among men—that should probably be a woman among women—but he couldn't concentrate on anything but battling nausea.

What on earth was she going to do all day? He should haul his sorry bones out of bed. He was wrecking her plans. This wasn't the holiday she'd signed up for.

'I'm spending the day at the beach, and it's going to be lovely,' she added as if she could read his mind. 'I'll see you later, Noah.'

He managed to croak out a 'Bye' before the door closed behind her.

It wasn't until she left that he suddenly realised she hadn't once met his eyes—not directly. He dragged himself upright, breathing hard, heart pounding. Sure, he'd been bleary eyed—and said eyes were probably bloodshot and hanging out of his head, so he wouldn't blame her for not wanting to look at them—but…that wasn't Bree's style. In fact, the more he thought about it, the more he realised she'd actively avoided making eye contact with him.

What the hell had he done last night?

He reached for the water, took two headache tablets.

Right… There'd been the beer, pizza, bourbon and crisps. They'd talked about heartbreak. He remembered that.

He scowled, a ferocious wave of something black and ugly making his hands clench. What he wouldn't give to rip Otis apart with his bare hands for having so utterly betrayed Bree. She hadn't deserved that. Nobody deserved that, but for some reason it seemed especially contemptible that Bree had been the victim of such a snake.

He ran a hand over his face. Although Courtney had left him at the altar, she hadn't gutted him the way Otis had Bree.

Well, of course not! The jerk had tried to make her his fall guy. She'd been arrested, for God's sake. Talk about a brutal wake-up call.

That didn't stem his growing unease. The fact remained, he couldn't relate to the heartbreak Bree had described. If he'd loved Courtney…

He pushed the thought away. Shock, he was

still in shock. Eventually it would wear off and no doubt he'd then experience in full Technicolor glory all that Bree had recounted. For the moment, though, he needed to focus on what mattered right now—Bree…and last night.

There'd been the game on the TV. He remembered Bree cheering a couple of times, but after that…?

His mind blanked. He'd obviously drunk himself into a stupor and passed out *on her bed*. He'd have not—

His mind flashed to a startlingly clear image of Bree leaning over him. He touched his fingers to his brow and fancied he could feel tingling warmth from the spot where she'd pressed her lips. She'd smelled so good—sweet like chocolate and fresh like night jasmine. He'd stared into those warm brown eyes, and had noticed the full promise of her plump bottom lip. In that precise moment, all he'd wanted to do was kiss her. He'd always thought her eyes extraordinary, but when the hell had he started noticing her lips?

His chest clenched. He'd wanted to kiss her, the need still burned through him and—

Hell! He hadn't…?

He lurched off the bed, just making it to the bathroom before losing the contents of his stomach.

Flushing the toilet and lowering the lid, he sat

on it, head in hands. He hadn't kissed Bree, had he? He'd never cross that boundary. No matter how drunk he was. Not with Bree.

But he had been *very* drunk.

If he hadn't kissed her—and he really didn't want to believe he'd kissed her—maybe he'd done something ridiculous like told her he wanted to kiss her. Because alcohol, as they all knew, was a truth serum.

He groaned out loud. Still, it would be the lesser of two evils. 'Never. Drinking. Again.'

Even if he hadn't behaved badly, last night couldn't have been fun for her. He needed to make that up to her somehow. First a shower, then some food, and then he'd make a plan.

Noah glanced across at Bree in the driver's seat. She'd insisted on driving the first leg of their journey to Sydney—a six-hour drive from Coffs Harbour. He'd barely seen her yesterday. Once she'd returned from her day at the beach, she'd excused herself to have an early night—had said she'd stayed up too late the previous night, and that all the sun, surf and fresh air had worn her out.

She hadn't looked worn out. She'd glowed from a day spent in the fresh air. A fact he'd done his very best not to notice. He told himself that the awareness he was starting to feel for her had to be some kind of weird hangover from being jilted at the altar.

It was probably some stupid male ego thing—his masculine pride wanting to reassert itself and prove he was still attractive and virile. To prove he was still worth something. As if pulling a girl proved anything.

As if taking advantage of a friend proved anything other than the fact he was worthless scum.

'I want to thank you, Bree.'

She started as if she'd been lost in her thoughts. She glanced at him briefly, eyebrows raised. 'What for?'

'You could've seriously punished me yesterday morning. You could've thrown the curtains open wide, turned the radio on loud and banged about the room. But you didn't. You brought me pain-killers, which was way more than I deserved. And you've not given me any grief over it since.'

'Why on earth would I want to punish you? And why would I give you grief?'

Please God, don't let him have given her any reason for either of those things.

'I don't think I know another woman who'd have acted the same way. Who'd have been so understanding.'

Her brows drew together. 'I had a pretty good idea what Saturday night was going to look like for you. After the day you'd had, nobody was going to blame you for drowning your sorrows, least of all me.'

'I stole your room.'

That made her laugh. 'What's a motel room between friends?'

He turned more fully towards her, careful not to knock the centre console with his knee. 'I know you just said you had no reason to have hard feelings, but I've got to ask—did I…behave badly towards you?'

'Whoa! Wait, *what*?' Her eyes went wide and a tiny bit panicked.

'Did I do something really stupid? Like, um… try to drunkenly kiss you?'

'I…*no*!' She shot him a wild-eyed glare before turning back to the road.

His nose curled at her…horror? Or was it repugnance? Did the idea of him kissing her revolt her that much?

'Hell, Noah, why would you even think such a thing?'

'Because you've been really quiet. I can't help thinking something's on your mind. And I get the feeling you're trying to avoid me.'

Stricken eyes met his. He swallowed. Was she lying to protect him? He had to have done something seriously bad to bring that expression to her eyes.

His gut churned but he kept his tone gentle.

'And I don't know if you've noticed or not, but we're in a car together. So avoiding me isn't going to work.'

She straightened, her knuckles white on the steering wheel. 'Lunch. It's lunchtime. I'm not having this conversation while I'm driving.'

They grabbed burgers, fries and shakes from the drive-thru of a fast-food chain and ate them at an all but deserted rest stop, where Noah hopefully wouldn't be recognised by anyone. They were closer to Sydney than Brisbane now and hopefully the cancelled wedding was of less interest the further south they went.

Bree bit into her burger and then closed her eyes and sipped her shake. He couldn't help feeling she was using the food as a way to keep avoiding him.

Catching his eyes, she shrugged. 'For the duration of the holiday I'm off the diet.'

His eyebrows shot up. 'In your normal day-to-day life you diet?'

'Not really.' She popped a couple of fries into her mouth. 'But I try to be mindful of what I eat. Still, holidays are for indulgences, right?'

He stared down at his food. He didn't want to think about indulgence. Not when Bree sat across from him with her plump bottom lip calling to him and the sun turning her hair the most delicious shade of ash blonde.

From the corner of his eye he saw her shrug. 'Still, I'll have to stop eating so much fast food, no matter how much I love it. Too many pizzas, burgers and chocolate bars will make me feel like crap, and there's still a long stretch of road between me and Hobart.'

'Then how about we indulge in some fine food rather than the fast variety when we're in Sydney?' It could be part of his make-it-up-to-her plan.

'Excellent idea.'

Her lips closed around her straw again and she darted a glance at him. He forced himself to not stare at her lips.

'Why did you ask if you'd kissed me?' she finally asked.

His gut churned. 'I can't remember if it was a real moment or whether I dreamed it, but I seem to recall a moment when I…uh, wanted to kiss you.'

He wasn't wearing a collared shirt, but a collar felt as if it were strangling him all the same. To Bree's credit, she didn't flinch or look the least bit appalled.

'Hand on my heart, Noah. You didn't try to kiss me, you didn't say anything inappropriate, you didn't do anything inappropriate.'

He sagged. Thank God for that. He picked up

his burger again, suddenly hungry. 'So you want to tell me why you've been avoiding me?'

She coughed as if food had gone down the wrong way. Setting his burger down, he gave her his full attention.

She dabbed her lips with a paper napkin—*those lips*—and then nodded as if coming to a decision. 'You were honest with me so…'

He'd been uncomfortably honest with her. And she looked just as uncomfortable now.

Her lips twisted. 'I suspect I'm about to raise an upsetting topic and I apologise in advance for that, but I think we better talk about it or I'll never be able to look you in the eye again.'

Hell!

'The thing is, Noah, I never for one moment thought you were really in love with Courtney.'

Things inside him stiffened, objected, protested and…agreed. His mouth dried.

'So on Saturday morning when we were all in the vestry and Courtney asked me what she did—whether I thought she should marry you or not—in my heart the answer was no.'

He could feel all the blood drain from his face as the truth descended on him with all the unpalatable weight of a T-Rex, which was what he felt like—an obsolete, outdated dinosaur.

'But after the things you said on Saturday night, I realise I was wrong—that you did love her. And rather than being bruised, your heart is in fact broken.

What on earth had he said on Saturday night to make her change her mind? He'd have asked except his throat had closed over.

Had he seriously been about to marry a woman he didn't love? He rubbed a hand over his face. He'd *thought* he'd been in love with Courtney, but now…

A wave of nausea rolled through him. Had he been so desperate to create his vision of the perfect life, the perfect family, he'd been prepared to marry a woman he didn't love?

Had he been that desperate to prove himself? So desperate he'd not only deceived her, but himself as well?

Except Courtney had seen through him. And so had Bree.

She pressed her hands together, her gaze pleading into his. 'Noah, I'm truly sorry for any assumptions I made, but I can fix this. If you want to win Courtney back, I can tell you exactly how to do it.'

CHAPTER FOUR

BREE STARED OUT of the passenger side window as they sped down the motorway, national park forest stretching on either side for as far as the eye could see, Noah's capable hands on the steering wheel and his forbidding *'No'* still ringing in her ears. That had been an hour and a half ago. In another hour they'd reach Sydney.

He hadn't explained why he'd said no—why he didn't want to win Courtney back. She couldn't work out if he loved the other woman or not. But if he did...

She twisted her hands together. If he did, she had to make him see that all wasn't lost.

If he didn't... The weight pressing down on her momentarily lifted. She *really* hoped he didn't.

One thing was becoming increasingly clear. She had to do something to cheer him up. Just a little. It would be impossible to entirely lift the darkness smothering him, but she could let in a chink of light, couldn't she?

But then what? Would he be okay on his own when she continued on with her journey? Should she stay with him for an extra few days?

She'd booked for three nights, but had no idea how long he planned to stay or where he was headed next. For all she knew he could be headed straight for the airport.

She wanted to ask what his plans were, but something held her back. She'd already infringed so much upon his privacy, it felt wrong to ask any more of him.

Besides, given the way he'd stared at her in the wee small hours of Sunday morning—the arc of awareness *that he remembered*—it was probably a very good thing the two of them part company. They were both trapped under heavy emotional loads at the moment and seeking relief.

That kind of relief, though, would be—

She shied away from even contemplating the consequences. It had the potential to ruin their friendship, destroy his relationship with her brothers and parents. His and Ryder's business would be affected...

She closed her eyes. She'd sworn to never let her family down again. Just for a moment she flashed to that cold impersonal courtroom and the grim white faces of her family.

Her eyes flew open. *No.* Sleeping with Noah would solve nothing, would ruin everything, and it would be letting everyone down. She couldn't bear it.

She couldn't use him like that. She *wouldn't* use him and sex as an escape from her panic for what her future held—panic that she wouldn't cope, that she wouldn't be enough. The step she was about to take meant sacrificing so many of the goals she'd spent the last seven years working towards.

She pulled in a breath, tried to temper the pounding of her heart. *But you'll be gaining so much as well.* She did all she could to hold fast to that thought. Because she would be. She'd be gaining the world.

But it didn't stop the dread, the nerves, the questions from circling through her mind on an endless loop. She craved a safety net...or a crystal ball that would let her see into the future and assure her all would be well.

She sensed Noah's quick glance in her direction and forced her mind back to the present moment. 'Would you like to do something fun while we're in Sydney?' she asked.

'What did you have in mind?'

She let out a slow breath at the interest that momentarily flickered in the backs of his eyes. She searched for something he might like to do. 'I've always wanted to do the bridge climb.'

He didn't look entirely thrilled at the prospect

and disappointment pooled in her stomach. Still, he hadn't immediately discounted it either so she pressed what little advantage she had. Getting him out in the fresh air and moving would do him the world of good.

'You make the most amazing fitness machines.' Noah provided the engineering genius behind Fitness Ark while Ryder was the business brain. Noah incorporated the latest fitness innovations and married them to virtual reality technology. People didn't go to Fitness Ark just to get fit—they went there for an experience. 'I wonder if you could make a machine that would recreate the bridge climb experience? You need to have a certain fitness level to do the climb. If you could recreate it with both surround video and sound…' She shrugged. 'It'd be pretty special.'

Everything about him went onto instant high alert.

'Eyes on the road,' she said when he swung to stare at her. She didn't speak again until he'd turned back to the front. 'It'd probably cost a lot of money to make that kind of machine. It could be prohibitively expensive. But it might be worth exploring.'

He didn't answer, but an entirely different mood settled in the car.

She fake pouted. 'I bet I've left it too late,

though. It's probably one of those things you need to book weeks in advance.'

'I'm sure I could organise something.'

Noah *knew* people. She pressed her hands together, her delight no longer feigned. 'Really?'

'Leave it to me, kiddo.'

His *kiddo* grated. She wasn't a kid any more and he knew it.

Maybe he was trying to set the same boundaries she'd been so desperate to find.

An unexpected thrill shook through her at the thought that Noah might find her attractive… even sexy. She did her best to suppress it, doing all she could to channel Bree-the-Serious-and-Sensible, rather than Bree-the-Wild-and-Reckless.

Something that became increasingly difficult to do when Noah turned towards the harbour rather than away from it when they reached the centre of Sydney. 'Noah, our hotel is that way.'

He shook his head, a faint smile curving his lips.

She dragged her gaze from that tempting mouth and pushed her phone under his nose. 'My navigation app says—'

'I made us other arrangements.'

Other arrangements? 'But—'

'Don't worry, I cancelled the reservation you'd made. You chose where we stayed in Coffs and paid for it. I figured it was only fair I did the same in Sydney.'

'But we're heading for the Rocks and a harbour view.'

'We are.'

Her mouth opened and closed when he pulled into one of the best hotels in the city. She'd have never stayed here in a month of Sundays. She'd have never been able to justify the expense.

He sent her a mock-stern glare. 'Don't rain on my parade here, Bree. You deserve a bit of pampering and so do I.'

He'd booked them a two-bedroom, harbour-view suite. When they walked in, she stared at the unbelievably luxurious furnishings and then the glorious view. 'This is amazing! Have you stayed here before?'

'A couple of times.'

She walked across to the window. 'I keep forgetting that you and Ryder could live like this if you wanted.'

His phone rang. He answered, listened and then nodded. 'Perfect. Thank you.'

What was perfect? And who was he thanking?

'That was the concierge. We're booked in for a sunset bridge climb tomorrow.'

She clapped her hands, bouncing from one foot to the other. 'That *is* perfect.'

'So?' He stared at her expectantly. 'What would you like to do this evening?'

It wasn't five p.m. yet. She stretched her neck to the right and then the left. 'We have a spa bath.' And the most glorious range of toiletries.

He laughed. 'After your spa, then, what would you like to do? If you're tired we can kick back here in the suite and order room service.'

She was tired. She'd forgotten how exhausting travelling could be, but while this room—suite—was about four times as big as both their rooms combined back in Coffs Harbour, it somehow seemed much more intimate.

Instinct warned her not to spend the evening in.

'Or I could see if I can get a reservation to Carlo's. I did promise you fine dining while we were here.'

Carlo's was considered one of the best restaurants in the country, and the mention of its name had Bree's mouth watering. But the photos she'd seen of the place had all screamed romance. The less romance she and Noah channelled at the moment, the better.

He was nursing a broken heart—or if it wasn't broken it was seriously bruised—and the last thing he needed was to be reminded of romance and all he'd lost.

As for her? She needed to get all the crazy,

wild thoughts she'd been having back under wraps. Fast. They were nothing more than a panicked reaction to the changes she was about to make in her life. If she wanted to prove to herself that she was worthy of the trust being placed in her, then she *had* to be sensible. If she couldn't do that, if she couldn't make good decisions now…

Then she didn't deserve anyone's trust.

Dragging in a breath, she made herself smile. 'You know what I'd really like to do? I'd like to go for a waterfront walk around to the Opera House. There are lots of eateries along the way. I'm sure we'd be able to find one that could fit us in without a booking. It's a Monday night so not exactly the busiest night of the week.'

He clapped his hands. 'Right, let's do that, then.'

The Sydney Harbour Bridge climb was amazing. Bree had known she'd enjoy it, but when they stood at the highest point and stared at the magnificence that was Sydney Harbour— surely one of the most beautiful sights in the world—exhilaration and adrenaline flooded her. A glance at Noah confirmed he felt the same.

'Best idea ever, Bree,' he breathed, awe and elation in every word.

'Make a machine that'll recreate this and I'll

be there every single day,' she murmured back, making him laugh.

After the bridge climb they returned to the hotel to get ready for dinner at Carlo's. She didn't know what strings Noah had pulled to get a table, but the thought of dining there was too tempting to resist.

And it lived up to expectation. While the atmosphere was intimate and warm, with candlelight and the sparkling lights of the harbour surrounding them, they were still too caught up in the exhilaration of the bridge climb to feel awkward. They simply talked non-stop the way they used to… BC—before Courtney. It made her realise how much she'd missed him. He was one of the few people she could let her guard down around and truly be herself.

She finally pushed her plate away and dabbed at her mouth with her pristine linen napkin. 'I can't eat another bite but that was the most spectacular meal I've ever eaten. It's been the best day.' She wiggled in her seat. 'I can't remember the last time I had this much fun.'

His gaze roved over her face and he nodded as if in approval. 'The night is yet young. What would else you like to do?'

'Heavens, I don't need anything else! Today has been such a treat and—'

'When was the last time you went dancing?'

Dancing? She couldn't remember. Ages and ages. She'd been so focussed on work and The Plan that dancing and going out hadn't been high on her list of priorities. 'I had a girls' night… um…a while back.'

Wow, it would be nearly a year ago.

His grin hooked up one side of his mouth. 'We don't have to be up early. We can laze around in the morning.'

She wasn't leaving Sydney till Thursday, and they hadn't made plans for tomorrow yet. A lie-in was definitely on the cards.

One broad shoulder lifted. 'I, for one, am still too revved to go back to our suite.'

A pulse thrummed to life inside her. She hadn't asked him yet what he planned to do once she set back off on her road trip.

The golden flecks in his eyes flashed. 'There's a club in a rather exclusive hotel not too far away. A mock-up of an old speakeasy. Are you up for it?'

She didn't hesitate. 'Yes, please.' Maybe she'd find the courage to ask him his plans over another glass of wine…find a way to ask without sounding too bossy or smothery.

As he promised, the place was full of character and old-world charm with a long wooden bar that dominated one wall. Round wooden tables and chairs surrounded a dance floor while beyond them banquettes lined the walls, creating dimly lit corners that looked as if they'd been designed for sealing shady bootlegging deals.

Nineteen-twenties music pulsed through the speakers and, even though it was a Tuesday night, dancers crowded the dance floor. When Noah grabbed her hand and hauled her out into the middle of all those bodies, she didn't resist.

Grinning at each other, they moved to the music in unison. As the beat pulsed through her and took up residence in the thrumming of her blood, she lifted her arms above her head, turned on the spot and shimmied, feeling young and free and more alive than she could remember feeling.

Noah's grin was full of the same wicked delight. He slipped an arm about her waist, his eyes gleaming with a mixture of mischief and appreciation. *Masculine* appreciation.

The breath stuttered in her throat as her arms lowered to his shoulders. He held her close as he whirled them around the dance floor and she did what she could to stifle the sensations flooding her body. Dear God, this couldn't be right. It—

All thought stopped when he dipped her over his arm and leaned down over her, so close she could see the fine pores of his face and the way the stubble darkened his jaw. Their gazes locked. Everything seemed to still and slow.

Very slowly he righted her, the fingers at her spine moving back and forth in an unconscious caress. Or maybe it was deliberate. All around them bodies moved, but they stood in the midst of it frozen, an island unto themselves. Bree couldn't look away, couldn't break the spell. Didn't *want* to break the spell.

A white flare made them both blink and start, but it took her several valuable seconds before she realised it was the flash of a camera going off in their faces rather than her hormones playing havoc.

A camera?

Noah moved in front of her, his body shielding hers—immediately protective.

Damn! The tabloid press had found them.

Outrage made her chest swell. Why couldn't the vultures leave Noah be and give him a chance to collect himself after the public humiliation of the cancelled wedding? They were like hyenas—going after a person when they were wounded. Well, she for one wasn't going to put up with it. Seizing his hand, she towed him towards an exit on the other side of the dance floor.

Outside in the corridor, she searched for a sign to the elevators. Damn it! They were only six floors up. Keeping a tight grip of his hand, she raced towards the fire escape.

'Not down there,' Noah said, taking the lead

and racing them around the corner instead. 'They're bound to have someone posted at the bottom.'

Devils. 'What are you looking for?'

'Staff service elevator.'

'Which way did they go?' a voice said not too far behind them. Footsteps approached.

It wasn't a service elevator, but... Pulling open the door of a storage cupboard, she dragged Noah inside and closed the door behind them, placing a finger against her lips. They heard whoever was following pass by and she let out a breath. While they might've given that particular photographer the slip, that didn't solve their problem of those who might be waiting downstairs.

Her heart plummeted when she glanced up at the stern set of Noah's mouth. This was so unfair. He deserved some peace.

She searched her mind for a solution when her gaze landed on a pile of neatly folded uniforms for the hotel's housekeeping staff. She tapped him on the shoulder and pointed. 'Nobody notices the staff.'

'Look, Bree, if I give them what they want you'll be able to slip into a taxi unnoticed and get back to our hotel unmolested.'

No way!

She picked up the nearest uniform and slapped it to his chest. 'Put this on.'

'And what do you suggest we do with our clothes?'

'There's a pile of laundry bags there. We'll put them in one of those. You can carry the laundry bag and we'll both carry room service trays with assorted bits and bobs on them. Nobody will be any the wiser.'

He hesitated.

'Do you want to talk to the press?' she demanded.

'Of course not.'

'Hurry, then. Change. And keep your back to mine. You don't need to know what colour my underwear is.'

This was foolhardy on so many levels, but Noah couldn't resist the fire in Bree's big brown eyes. There was a spirit, a vehemence, in their depths that he hadn't seen since...

Since Otis, he suddenly realised. It had been too long returning and he wasn't going to be the one to dim it.

He *loved* seeing it back there. It made her entire being come alive. An answering fire flashed through him. She was right. He didn't have to let the press walk all over him.

An entirely different spark flashed through him when her arm—her *naked* arm—brushed against his. And then her hip. This room might be generous in terms of storage space, but it was far too small for two people to be undressing in simultaneously.

Don't think about the undressing!

Gritting his teeth, he pulled his shirt from his waistband and undid the buttons. He had it half-way down his arms, doing his best not to bump up against Bree too much, when the door to the storage room was wrenched open and a series of bright flashes half blinded him.

Hell!

He moved in front of Bree in an effort to shield her, but he was too late. A glance over his shoulder showed him shocked wide eyes. She clasped her blouse to her chest. The hot pink straps of her bra gleamed bright against the honey of her skin, and the sight of her had him biting back a groan of pure unadulterated desire. With a swift oath, he shoved the camera back outside and slammed the door, before locking it.

'I didn't lock it,' she whispered. 'How could I have been so stupid as to not lock the door?'

The sparkle had well and truly disappeared and his gut dropped to the soles of his feet. How could he have let this happen? He'd let her down. He'd let the entire Allenby family down.

'Plan B,' he ground out.

'Which is?'

He hated how small her voice had gone. She

didn't rail at him for getting her into this mess, but her silence was a hundred times worse. 'I ring Security and they escort us out a back way unseen.'

'Okay.'

They were back in their own suite forty minutes later. She turned to him the moment the door shut behind them. 'What now?'

He had to do everything he could to protect her from further media attention. 'We leave at the crack of dawn and disappear—find some out-of-the-way place between here and Melbourne and go to ground for a few days.'

Her face fell. 'You're coming to Melbourne?'

His temples throbbed. 'I know I'm messing with your plans, Bree, and I'll try to get out of your hair as soon as I can, but—'

'I'm not worried about that!'

She wasn't?

'I'm just sorry the press are hassling you and not giving you a chance to…' She shrugged. 'You know?'

Yeah, he knew, but she always put everyone before herself. Regardless of what she said, he was screwing with her plans and her desire for a leisurely, relaxing holiday.

His hands clenched. He'd do everything in his power to mitigate the damage he'd caused. 'I'm going to talk to the hotel manager—just in case the press finds out where we're staying, and no doubt they will. I might need to organise a decoy for the morning.'

'A decoy?'

'An official-looking car—maybe a limo—with blacked-out windows and a driver who might happen to whisper in an ear or two that he's been hired to drive me and a friend to the airport.'

'Wow. Okay.'

'Can you be ready to leave at six in the morning?'

She nodded. 'Is there anything else I can do?'

He glanced at the clock. She'd be lucky to get three or four hours' sleep. 'Nah, I've got it covered.' He did what he could to keep his tone light, jolly even, but it didn't chase the shadows from her eyes. 'I'll see you in the morning, Bree.'

He strode away, wanting to swear and swear and swear.

The shadows hadn't disappeared from her eyes the next day, not even after they'd left Sydney far behind. The sparkle had gone, leaving them dull and flat.

For the first hour and a half she'd sat hunched in the passenger seat, staring dully out of the window. She hadn't put up an argument when he'd said he'd like to take the first driving shift, had just handed the car keys over without a murmur.

He gripped the steering wheel so tight his fingers started to ache, before setting the cruise control to stop inadvertently speeding. 'You okay over there?'

She forced herself to un-hunch—at least, that was how it seemed to him. As if rousing herself took a giant effort. 'Sure I am.' She sent him a weak smile that didn't reach her eyes. 'What about you?'

He deserved to burn in hell for dragging her into this mess. 'I'm fine.'

He could tell she didn't believe him, so he rushed on. 'You want to know the plan?'

She straightened some more. 'Yes, please.'

'I've booked accommodation for a few nights at a farm-stay place on the other side of Albury Wodonga. It does mean driving for six hours again today, but if it gets the press off our tails...'

'It'll be well worth it,' she finished for him.

'It's called the Colonial Cheese Factory. Check it out on your phone. It's kind of quaint.' The moment he'd seen the pictures he'd known she'd love it.

He'd hoped it would bring a smile to her lips, so was disappointed when she merely read out the website information. She nodded. 'It looks pretty private, except...'

His gut clenched. 'Except?'

'It says they cater for couples and family

groups as well as larger gatherings. If they have other people staying there at the moment then our cover could be blown.'

'Nobody else is staying there or booked to stay there. I checked. We're halfway between Easter and the next lot of school holidays, and they said they're ridiculously quiet.' He'd made sure it would stay that way by booking out the entire venue.

She closed her phone. 'Sounds perfect, then.'

She'd made no mention of getting a chance to milk a cow or collect fresh eggs or…anything. 'They have baby chicks.'

She glanced at him, the tiniest hint of interest brightening her eyes. 'Cute, fluffy yellow chicks?'

He nodded, suppressing a smile. 'And piglets.'

Her eyes widened. 'Piglets? Oh, that sounds fun. I wonder if we'd be allowed to pet them… play with them.'

'We can. I checked. Because you're right.' He laughed. 'How could piglets not be fun?'

To his relief she laughed too. 'What's more,' he added, 'they'll also provide us with canoes to go bobbing about on the river if we want. Far away from prying eyes,' he said with relish in his voice when she looked less convinced by that plan. 'Silently gliding on the water… I can't remember the last time I went canoeing.'

She stared at him. 'You sound like you miss it?'

Her words made him blink. 'I guess I have. I didn't realise how much until our hosts mentioned it was one of the activities available. Their property backs onto the river.'

'You make it sound nice. We should definitely do that while we're there.'

He felt the weight of her stare and turned to meet it briefly. He opened his mouth, but she continued. 'You know, Noah, we can spend an extra night or two here if we want. There's plenty of time before I have to board the overnight ferry for Tassie.'

For the moment he was just happy to see a little colour in her cheeks. 'Let's just play it by ear, shall we?' Neither of them had checked the newspaper headlines yet. The moment she saw those she might want to kick his sorry butt to the kerb.

It made no sense, but the thought of that drilled into his soul, making him ache in a way not even Courtney's rejection at the altar had.

He clenched his jaw. Oh, it made sense all right. All the sense in the world. He hadn't loved Courtney while the Allenbys meant everything to him. The thought of them turning their backs on him made him sick to the stomach. He glanced across at Bree. Her shoulders had started to hunch again.

'Okay…' he tapped his fingers against the steering wheel '…game time.'

She shifted towards him. 'Game?'

'I'm sorry, Bree, but if I have to listen to any more ABBA I'm going to go mad. I'm driving so I get to make up the rules.'

She huffed out a laugh at that and he refused to question the spark of energy it sent racing through him.

'We're going to play the alphabet band game,' he announced. 'We go through the alphabet—A through to Z—and name a band starting with the letter. We can't name the same band.'

She straightened. 'I up your "band" game to the "band and song" game. The song doesn't have to come from the same band, but you get extra points if it does.'

'Game on!'

'I get to go first,' she said, too quickly for him to counter. 'A for ABBA and "Arrival".'

'"Arrival" isn't a song, it's—'

'Of course it is. It's the name of an album *and* a song. That means I should get triple quadruple points.'

'It's not a song. It's an instrumental piece.'

'You really want to be that picky?'

'I'm driving. My rules.'

He kept his gaze on the road ahead, but sensed

her bristling beside him—all fired up and competitive. He grinned.

'Fine! A for ABBA and "Andante Andante". Ha! Bonus points are mine.'

'Air Supply and "Air That I Breathe",' he shot back immediately. 'And I get extra bonus points for getting the word Air in both the band and the song.'

A laugh gurgled out of her. 'You great big fat cheat! Anyway it's "*The* Air That I Breathe!"' Which made him laugh too.

It should've been a bad day—a really bad day. But he'd enjoy this bubble of fun while it lasted.

Noah blew out a breath. 'Are you ready?'

They sat beneath the large pergola behind the factory part of the Colonial Cheese Factory, which housed a huge dining room on the ground floor and dormitory-style accommodation above. Their quarters were in a surprisingly large two-bedroom unit. Two of these formed a wing that extended behind the factory, with the pergola filling the space between.

The owners had a separate house at the front of the property while an additional six cabins marched down towards the river. It was private, secluded and very beautiful.

They'd nursed cute baby chicks, made friends with the milking cow, petted a huge Shire horse and hugged squirming piglets delighted to find in them new playmates.

Bree tossed a handful of seed, from the supply they'd been given, and two magnificent peacocks swooped in to gobble it up.

He shook his head. 'I can't believe they have peacocks.'

'They do seem a bit of an anomaly,' she agreed. 'But a nice one.' She dragged in a breath. 'Okay, I suppose I have to see it some time, and I guess I'm as ready as I'm ever going to be.'

He wished he could spare her this. He wished he could spare them both.

With fingers that weren't quite steady, he loaded the article, complete with those scandalous photos, onto his tablet and then held it out for her to see. He'd read it earlier—had tried to prepare her for it.

Even though she'd steeled herself, she still flinched. He wanted to hurl the tablet into the hydrangea bushes on the other side of the drive. Instead, he let her pluck it from his hands to read the article. He shooed away one of the peacocks when it started pecking a little too close to her sneaker.

'They... I knew... But—'

Her pallor made him wince.

'I knew they'd make it seem like we were having a torrid affair,' she finally choked out. 'But...

oh, God. They make it sound like I broke you and Courtney up!'

'I know, Bree. But we know the truth and so do the people who matter—your family. And any of our friends worth their salt will too.'

She nodded, misery etched in the lines of her mouth. 'I'm so sorry, Noah. This is all my fault!'

His head rocked back. 'What are you talking about?'

'If I hadn't talked you into trying to disguise ourselves that awful photo would never have been taken. And I don't know how to make things right. I rang Mum and Dad, Ryder and Blake the night it happened so they'd all know this wasn't your fault. And if I'd had Courtney's number I'd have done the same. I can still—'

'Why on earth would you want to ring Courtney?'

'To tell her the truth!' She gestured at the photo. 'You're never going to be able to make things right with her if she believes this garbage.'

'Why would I want to make things right with her?'

'Because you love her!'

What the hell…?

He stared at Bree and shook his head. 'I don't love Courtney, Bree.' He enunciated the words clearly. 'I don't think I ever did.'

CHAPTER FIVE

'ARE YOU SERIOUS?'

Was Noah telling her the truth? He really wasn't in love with Courtney? Some of the awful weight that had been pressing down on Bree's chest lifted.

He frowned. 'Of course I'm serious.'

That weight lifted even further.

'I'm *not* in love with Courtney.'

Reaching over, he reclaimed his tablet and switched it off before setting it on the table. She had a feeling he only did it to give himself something to do, an excuse to not meet her eyes.

The weight pressed back down. Was he lying?

Eventually he lifted his head, his gaze direct even as his eyes swirled with myriad different emotions. 'I'm not in love with Courtney.' His shoulders slumped. 'I realised that the moment I woke up with the hangover I deserved in Coffs Harbour.'

The weight disappeared for good. She wanted

to jump up and cheer. *Entirely inappropriate, Bree.* She dragged in a breath. *Stay in your seat; keep your expression calm.*

'I thought you knew that.' His frown deepened. 'I thought…' One broad shoulder lifted. 'Once I had the time to consider it all in a halfway logical manner, I thought what happened in the vestry—with you refusing to tell Courtney we were well suited—proved you'd recognised the truth long before I did.'

'What made you realise you weren't in love with her?'

He hesitated for a fraction of a second. 'You telling me about how you'd felt when things exploded between you and Otis.'

Oddly, Otis's name didn't make her flinch as it usually did.

'Courtney dumping me at the altar shocked me, and the rejection stung me right down to my bone marrow, but I'm ashamed to admit I was more concerned with what everyone would think than I was with why Courtney had decided to run.' He rubbed a hand over his face. 'I owe her an apology of epic proportions.'

He pulled his hand away. 'But you knew then, right, at the wedding?'

She half nodded, half shrugged. 'At the time I was convinced. I knew you *thought* yourself in love with her. But if you'd truly loved her nothing would've stopped you from going after her and trying to make things right.'

He glanced down at his hands. 'I should've told her I loved her when we were in the vestry, and then she'd have stayed and married me. That's what you meant, wasn't it, when you said earlier that I could still make things right?'

She nodded. 'Do you wish you had?'

He shook his head. 'It would've been a lie, a terrible lie, but I have an awful feeling I'd have said it anyway to save us from the embarrassment of cancelling the wedding—to save face. How shallow is that?' He glanced up, his eyes dark and shadowed. 'It makes me sick to the stomach just thinking about it. Who the hell have I become that I'd hurt someone so badly just to save myself from feeling humiliated?'

She gripped his hand. 'It makes you human like the rest of us. At the time you wouldn't have thought you were lying. You would've thought you were fixing things and making them right.'

The smile he sent her pierced her heart. 'I thought marrying Courtney would prove that I'd finally made it—that I was a success, not just in my business life, but in my private life as well. But it turns out I'm no better than my parents after all.'

She shot to her feet and the peacocks started

like maidens in a gothic horror movie, picking up their skirts and racing away. She clenched her hands so hard she started to shake. 'Don't you ever say that again! It's not true and hearing you say it makes me want to slap you harder than I've ever wanted to slap anyone in my whole entire life.'

To her horror, her eyes filled and a sob gathered in the back of her throat. She swallowed it down. 'Not that I ever would, of course. I'd never hit anyone, but I'd definitely never lift a hand against *you*.'

'Bree.' He rose too, his face gentling. 'Don't do this. Don't you think I know that?'

And then she found herself pulled into his arms and she was breathing in his warm, comforting scent so familiar to her. Except the breadth of his chest and the strength of his arms and the lean power she felt coursing through him as she wrapped her arms around him was far from familiar. And it had awareness flooding through her.

She revelled in it for a couple of delicious breaths and then eased away because she couldn't stay there, no matter how much she might want to. His arms tightened briefly before releasing her.

Taking her hand, he made her sit again and sat back down beside her. Did she imagine it or had he shifted closer? 'Bree, I know you didn't mean it literally.'

Given how fast and ready his parents had been with their fists, though, her comment had been far from sensitive.

'You've been my champion since you were a feisty eight-year-old.'

When she was eight and Noah eleven, his family had moved into a house one street over from the Allenbys. Bree had been riding her bike on the footpath one summer afternoon when Noah, with his father in hot pursuit, had come bolting out of the house. Mr Fitzgerald had grabbed Noah by the arm and had started laying into him with the nearest thing to hand—a fence paling.

She'd been so outraged she'd leapt off her bike and run at Mr Fitzgerald yelling she was going to call the police. Mr Fitzgerald had been so surprised he'd let Noah go.

Noah had immediately leapt in front of her as if to protect her from his father's wrath, but she'd had no intention of sticking around. She'd grabbed Noah's hand and they'd run all the way back to her place. She'd thrown herself into her mother's arms and had sobbed out the whole story.

Her mother had fed them cookies and milk, had taken care of Noah's bruises and grazes, and had talked to them in her usual even tones until Bree's fright had eased.

She never knew what her mother and father said to Noah's parents later that afternoon, but Noah said it had made them stop hitting him.

Instead they'd vacillated between verbal abuse and ignoring him completely. As far as Bree was concerned, they were scum of the earth. The moment Noah had finished Year Twelve they'd turned him out of the house, claiming they'd done their duty. She didn't think he'd ever spoken to them again. They'd moved six years ago.

And good riddance! The Allenbys were Noah's family now. That first evening, her mother had made up a bed for Noah in the twins' room and he'd stayed with them for three whole nights. At the end of which he'd been firmly established as an honorary member of the Allenby clan. It had been understood by all parties from that time on that Noah would attend Sunday night family dinners. Or else.

Her parents had also taken Bree aside and told her she was to never step foot inside the Fitzgerald yard again. They'd made her promise. Considering the incident now from the ripe old age of twenty-six, she could appreciate how many grey hairs she must've given her parents over that incident.

'I'm glad I was riding past your house that day,' she said.

His hand tightened about hers. 'Me too.'

She turned to face him more fully, swallowing when she realised how close his face was to hers. 'You're nothing like your parents, Noah. *Nothing.* And—'

'They were selfish.' His face hardened. 'What they wanted mattered far more than anything else. And in this instance I've been just as selfish. I wanted this idealistic life with the perfect woman, and I went after it with a single-minded focus that didn't take her needs or wants into account.'

'What are you talking about? You didn't compel Courtney to accept your proposal. You gave her every damn thing that she wanted.'

'Except my heart.'

Her stomach dropped to her toes. 'Oh, Noah. You'd have given her that too if you could've.'

'What I did...now feels heartless. I didn't mean to hurt anyone, but that doesn't change the fact that I did. I'm ashamed of myself, sickened at what I've done.'

She pulled in a breath. 'You made a mistake. It doesn't mean you're a bad person.'

She hesitated. He leaned towards her. 'Go on.'

'I just think...rather than being ashamed of where you've come from—your background—

you should be proud of where you are now and all you've achieved. You've been hell-bent on creating some mythically perfect life for yourself, but have you actually asked yourself if it'd truly make you happy?'

He stared at her but remained silent, so she forged on. 'It seems to me that you've been living in the future in an attempt to vanquish the past.' She spread her hands. 'But what about the here and now? Shouldn't you be relishing it?'

He sat back with a shake of his head, the faintest of smiles touching his lips. 'When did you get so wise and deep? But…' His lips pursed. 'Maybe you're onto something. I've been so focussed on trying to prove something to myself—'

He broke off, hauled in a breath. 'It's going to take some thinking through. One thing is for certain, I sure as hell haven't been living in the moment.'

Maybe that was something she *could* help with. 'What *are* your plans now, Noah? Short-term, I mean. I know Ryder wanted you to keep a low profile until he could clinch the Fullerton deal, which I figured meant you staying out of Brisbane for the next few weeks. What were you planning to do in Sydney?'

'I didn't have a plan. I just didn't want to cramp your style for too long and Sydney was the biggest place on your itinerary. Seemed a good place to lose myself in for a while.'

She moistened suddenly dry lips. 'Why don't you come to Tassie, then, and do something you love while you're there?' She searched her mind. 'Like white-water rafting or… Tasmania has wildlife treks that sound amazing. You know the spiel—treks through the world's most southernmost temperate rainforest or pristine marine reserves. We're talking truly remote World Heritage locations. That would be right up your alley.'

The amber flecks in his eyes flashed. She'd never thought the word hazel captured their beauty. They deserved a better description… like forest gold.

'Or,' she improvised, 'maybe you could crew on a yacht heading back up the coast. Bass Strait is notoriously tricky and might provide you with one of those adrenaline rushes you seem to enjoy. Besides, it'd be hard for the press to find you if you're deep in virgin forest or out at sea.'

That made him laugh. 'I like both of those ideas. A lot. I'll do some research tonight.' He stared at her for a long moment. 'Are you sure you don't mind me tagging along?'

'Not at all.' In fact, she'd enjoyed having him along. She fought back a frown. Perhaps she'd been enjoying it a little too much. She *was* supposed to be focussing on the future, after all.

'You know I'm going to ask you again, why you're heading to Hobart?'

Who knew, maybe she'd even tell him? 'But not tonight.'

His mouth opened as if he meant to argue, but their host chose that moment to step outside from the quirky factory behind them. 'Your dinner is ready. Just let me know when you'd like to eat it and—'

Bree leapt up. 'Normally we eat much later, but now will be fabulous.' It was an hour and a half earlier than her usual dinnertime, but… She glanced at Noah. 'I'm starving, aren't you?' They'd barely eaten anything all day. 'We set off so early this morning.'

'Famished.' He rose too.

'I'll make you up a cheese and fruit platter to take back to your apartment to nibble on later?'

'Better and better,' Bree said with a smile that felt oddly light and free. 'I have a feeling we're going to enjoy our stay here very much, Mrs Wilks.'

They were served huge bowls of the most delicious cassoulet she'd ever eaten, along with generous chunks of warm crusty bread. When the worst of their hunger had been sated, and Bree was wiping a piece of the bread through the gravy left in her bowl, because she couldn't bear to waste any of it even though she was now full, she glanced up to find Noah watching her. 'What?' Did she have food smeared across her face? She hastily wiped her mouth with a napkin.

'You figured out early on that I wasn't in love with Courtney. What made you change your mind?'

She pushed her plate away. 'You seemed so gutted on Saturday night, and when we talked about heartbreak and Otis, I realised I had absolutely no right to leap to conclusions about you and your situation.'

He shook his head, pushing his plate away too. 'You do, you know? We're friends, Bree. We've known each other a long time. Leap to all the conclusions you want. I don't mind.'

She couldn't smile, even though she knew he wanted her to. 'That thing that happened with the tabloids, despite what you say, Noah, it was my fault. Dragging us into that storage cupboard and donning disguises… It was a stupid thing to do.'

'It didn't feel stupid. It felt like we were taking back power. It felt like an adventure.'

She'd given him no say in the matter—had just ordered him about. 'And look what happened. I made things worse for you. And Ryder is now having to do double-duty damage control in Brisbane.'

Her stomach churned and she wished she hadn't eaten so much. 'It threw me back to my crazy wild days with Otis and we all know how well that turned out. I let everyone down back then and I felt like I'd let you down again last night. And if you'd still been in love with Courtney I'd have ruined things utterly.'

'Bree—'

'I felt like I'd screwed everything up for everyone. And I've been trying so hard not to be that person.'

It was of paramount importance that she not ever be that person again. Her very reason for going to Hobart…the discussions she and Tina were about to have…the outcome of those discussions…it all relied on her no longer being rash and irresponsible. She couldn't let Tina and her daughter Tilly down, or Tina's parents. The very thought had acid burning her throat.

Noah's hand on hers brought her back to the present. 'Bree, you're no longer the same person you were then. You've grown up, matured, and you've learned from your mistakes. You need to be proud of all you've achieved too.'

She wanted to believe him, but she didn't believe in fairy tales. Not any more.

Noah dipped the paddle in the water and slid the canoe over the surface of the river, letting the natural beauty filter into his soul. Gum trees—mostly grey and ghost gums—lined the opposite bank while native undergrowth provided thick cover for the wildlife. He picked out the chatter of parrots, the distinctive call of a butcherbird and a warbling magpie.

As he closed his eyes calm flooded his soul. The raucous laughter of three kookaburras had him opening them again a little while later with a smile.

He glanced across at Bree, who rested her paddle crossways on her canoe and just let it drift, a dreamy expression on her face. He let out a slow breath, noting her shoulders had lost some of their tension.

He'd barely been able to believe what he'd heard last night. Bree wasn't a screw-up. He couldn't believe she saw herself as one. Nobody in her family saw her as anything but smart, driven…and kind. He'd said as much. The twist of her lips, though, had told him his words had made little impact.

What had happened with Otis had changed her. It had made her more careful, less carefree, more focussed on her work. It had hurt him, seeing those changes, but he'd understood them, understood her need to feel safe again. He just hadn't realised she'd blamed herself so completely for being taken in by Otis.

For heaven's sake, she'd only been nineteen and in her second year of university when she'd

met and tumbled head over heels in love with
Otis Collins. She'd had crushes before, but they'd
all sensed that Otis was different. None of them
had realised that beneath his 'good guy' persona
Otis had been dealing drugs to fund his growing cocaine habit.

Hell! He'd attended every single Sunday
night family dinner that Bree had invited him
to, unlike some other persons who would remain
nameless.

Even when Bree had started partying too hard
and her grades had started to suffer, they'd all put
it down to youthful high spirits. Her horror when
she'd flunked one of her subjects had reassured
them all that she'd get some balance back in her
life and knuckle down to her studies.

They'd all been blind. Not to Bree—they'd
read her perfectly. But blind to Otis. The police,
thankfully, hadn't been so naïve or so trusting.
They'd been keeping tabs on Otis for months
and it was during a surprise raid on his house
that Otis had slipped a significant amount of cocaine into Bree's handbag. When it was discovered, Otis had claimed Bree was the dealer and
he was her patsy.

Of course, Bree's fingerprints were nowhere
to be found on the drugs and her drug tests
came back negative, unlike Otis's. But she'd
spent a night in a jail cell. She'd had to testify in

court. Even now Noah could recall her pinched white face and the dark circles beneath her eyes, blue as bruises. For as long as Noah lived, he never wanted to see that expression again on her face. He'd do anything in his power to prevent it.

Otis, though, was to blame for all of that. Not her.

She'd admitted later that she'd known Otis occasionally took drugs and he had laughed at her concern, but he'd promised to stop and she'd believed him. She'd had no idea that his drug use had escalated or that he'd become a dealer.

She'd made a mistake in trusting Otis and that was hardly a crime.

The ringtone of her phone sounded from the riverbank—ABBA's 'Mamma Mia', of course—weirdly cheerful amid all of this bucolic serenity.

She glanced at him as he paddled up beside her. 'If this was a normal day in a normal week,' she said with a sigh, 'I'd ignore it.'

But it wasn't. Every time one of their phones rang, they tensed.

'I'll check it quickly and be right back.' She gestured around at the view. 'This is too glorious to be away from for too long.'

He watched her paddle back to the sandy shore and pull her canoe up beneath the trailing fronds of a pepper tree. She checked her phone and frowned. 'It's work,' she called out. 'I better call them back.' She punched in a number and then held it to her ear. She strode the length of the small beach to the weeping willow that marked its other end.

He couldn't hear what she said. She seemed to be doing more listening than speaking. The call was brief. When it was over she stowed her phone back with their picnic basket and other bits and pieces they'd brought down to the bank with them and pushed back out towards him.

He tensed at the angry glitter in her eyes. 'Everything okay? They haven't cancelled your leave, have they?' She'd not taken a proper holiday in an age. She deserved a break.

'I've been fired.'

'What?'

He stiffened so suddenly his canoe rocked and she reached across to steady it. 'Careful. You don't want to take a dip. The water's cold.'

He reached out to grab the side of her canoe to prevent her from paddling away. 'Why?'

She blew out a breath and glanced skyward. It was a perfect blue—he'd already checked.

'It was that damn tabloid article, wasn't it?'

'In a way.' She huffed out a mirthless laugh. 'Courtney's father bought the practice this morning.'

Bree worked for a large physiotherapy practice

that specialised in sporting injuries and post-op recuperation.

'His first action as the new owner was to fire me.'

Courtney's father had bought the physiotherapy practice with the sole purpose of…

'If you overturn my canoe, Noah, I'm going to be seriously unimpressed.'

He loosened his grip, but his heart thundered in his chest. 'That is—' he started through gritted teeth. 'I—'

'It doesn't matter. I actually qualify for a rather attractive redundancy package.'

He sucked air into his lungs and forced himself to let it out slowly. 'You can bring your plan to open your own practice forward.' They all knew The Plan off by heart, they'd heard it so many times. Graduate with a double degree by the ripe old age of twenty-two. Work for several years gaining valuable experience while saving hard. Open her own practice by the time she was thirty, but ideally by age twenty-eight. She was twenty-six now. It was only twenty months early.

Her gaze slid away. 'The time's not right for that.'

He didn't ask why. She'd have a sound reason. 'Good.'

Her eyebrows flew up and she glanced back at him.

'It means I can table an offer Ryder and I have been wanting to extend to you.'

'Offer?'

'We've held off because we knew The Plan and your dream of opening your own clinic, being your own boss.' He shrugged. 'We get it. We both wanted to be our own bosses too, and we haven't wanted to pressure you to give up that dream.'

'Offer?' she said again.

'You know that Ryder and I plan to expand our gyms?'

She nodded. 'You've plans to open franchises in Sydney, Melbourne and Adelaide.'

'We don't just want to expand into new locations. We want to increase the services we offer.'

She stared at him expectantly.

He spread his hands wide. 'Like a physiotherapy clinic and the opportunity for appointments with a dietician. Your double degree plus the business training you've done on the side makes you the perfect candidate to head up that side of operations.'

Her jaw dropped. She leaned towards him. 'Are you making that up on the fly or have you and Ryder really talked about this?'

'Hand on heart.' He clapped a hand to his chest. 'We're still in discussions. He thinks we should table you an offer.'

'And you?'

Her voice had gone husky and it brushed against the nerve endings of his skin, firing things to life inside him. 'I don't want you to give up your dreams to help us achieve ours. But one of Ryder's arguments is beginning to hold weight with me. He says just because we make you an offer doesn't mean you have to accept it, that having options is always a positive thing.'

Her lips lifted. 'That sounds like Ryder.' Her eyes started to sparkle. 'It sounds really exciting! I'd be building it from the ground up and—'

She broke off, her eyes losing that sparkle.

'What?' he barked, wanting the sparkle back.

'The timing's not right.'

'Why not? If you're between jobs and it's not the right time to open your own clinic…?'

She rubbed both hands over her face. 'The thing is, Noah, The Plan has changed.'

She'd changed The Plan? He blinked, frowned. Why was this the first he'd heard of it? *Why* had she changed it? It was *seriously* out of character. 'Is this because you've been fired?'

'No, not because of that.'

She smiled but it was full of a sadness he didn't understand.

'C'mon.' She hitched her chin in the direction of the bank. I don't want you capsizing our canoes. This is a conversation for dry land... and chocolate.'

He followed her back to the shore, skimming past her to heave both canoes up onto the bank and then offering his hand to help her out. She gripped his hand and stood, and then glanced up into his face and stilled at whatever she saw there. She pressed a hand to his cheek. 'Don't look so worried, Noah.'

She pulled her hand away and his skin burned from where she'd touched it. He wanted to grab her hand and put it back. He wanted her to keep staring into his eyes with that same soft warmth. He wanted—

Stop it.

Choking down the inconvenient attraction, he followed her to the picnic blanket. 'How can I not worry? It sounds serious.'

'It is serious.' She knelt on the blanket and rifled through the picnic hamper their hostess had provided for them. 'It's serious, sad...exciting...terrifying.'

She settled back with a chocolate bar and pulled off the wrapper. Breaking off a piece, she tossed it to him before popping a second piece into her mouth and gesturing for him to take a seat.

'So, you know Tina,' she started.

He suppressed the instinct to pace and forced himself down to the blanket, popping the piece of chocolate into his mouth with an equanimity he was far from feeling. 'Tina who you're visiting in Hobart? Best friends forever and all that. What about her?'

Bree and Tina had been inseparable until the end of Year Ten when Tina's parents had relocated to Hobart. The girls had kept in constant contact. They'd holidayed together at different times—while they were still at school, with each other's families. When they were at university they'd catch up whenever they could. With the recent concerns about Tina's health, Bree had made multiple trips to Hobart in the last couple of years.

'Blake has a theory you've met some guy in Tassie and that's why you've been visiting so often.'

'I wish that were the case. I really do.'

But her sigh said otherwise and his every sense went on high alert.

'Tina's brain tumour has returned.'

He sucked in a breath. Tina had undergone major surgery two years ago.

'There's nothing they can do. Initially they were hopeful that radiation treatment would keep it under control, but…'

She trailed off and his throat burned at the sadness in her eyes. 'How long has she got?'

'Best-case scenario is eighteen months.'

Hell. Life could be so unfair. 'I'm sorry, Bree.'

She nodded. 'It sucks.'

'You've been trying to spend as much time with her as you can?'

'Absolutely.' She glanced up, even more downcast if that were possible. 'And Tilly is only three.'

Tilly was Tina's daughter. 'And as Tilly's godmother you want to be there for her.'

Some little kid was now going to grow up without her mother. His hand's clenched. 'Tilly's father…?'

'He shot through when Tina was pregnant. He wanted nothing to do with either of them.'

He swore.

'Tina's parents are in their sixties. They had Tina when they were in their early forties.'

She stared at him half expectantly, but he didn't know what she was waiting for. 'They must be beside themselves,' he murmured.

'Gutted.' She glanced down at her hands. 'She's an only child—no brothers or sisters.'

No wonder Bree had been visiting so regularly. No doubt she was helping out wherever and however she could; offering all the emotional support Tina, Tilly and Tina's parents needed. 'Why haven't you told any of us about this before now, Bree?' They could've at least given her whatever emotional support *she* needed.

She moistened her lips. He refused to notice their shine in the warm autumn sunshine. Or how they beckoned and sent a summer heat curling through him.

'Tina and Tilly don't really have anyone, Noah. I mean, Tina has friends—plenty of them—but none like me. We're practically sisters…and with her parents getting on…'

What on earth was she trying to tell him?

'Tina wants Tilly raised by a young woman like herself. She doesn't want her parents running themselves ragged in their later years when they should be enjoying their retirement.'

He stared. He couldn't utter a single word.

'She's asked if I'll be Tilly's guardian.'

He should've seen this coming. How could he have been so slow-witted?

'And I've said yes.'

CHAPTER SIX

BREE HELD HER breath after she delivered her life-changing piece of news. Maybe she imagined it, but for three beats of her heart everything went still—even the birds stopped singing—but then it all seemed to rush back at her with ten times the force.

Breathe, Bree, breathe.

'You're going to raise Tilly?'

She shoved more chocolate in her mouth and nodded.

She watched his every expression with an eagle-eyed concentration, waiting for concern, consternation…opposition. Opposition that she didn't have the ability to do it, that she wouldn't be able to provide Tilly with a stable home—that she was too ill equipped, selfish, and irresponsible to be trusted with such a role. That she was too much of a screw-up to ever be a maternal role model for anyone.

Instead, those extraordinary amber flecks in

his eyes blazed gold and she blinked, momentarily dazzled. 'You are your mother's daughter.'

Her eyes filled. It was the biggest compliment he could give anyone.

'You're brave and true and so committed to the people you love. You have such a big heart, Bree, and I'm beyond awed that you've chosen to share all of that with Tilly—to provide her with all the love and security that she's going to need.'

He was?

'It's tragic that she's losing her mother at such a young age. But she has you and that makes her lucky.'

She did what she could to dislodge the lump in her throat. 'You don't think it's a crazy idea?'

'Not for a moment.' He leaned towards her. 'I'll do everything in my power to support you. Your whole family will.'

His words made her heart clench. 'I know. It's just... I'm terrified.'

It was liberating to admit it out loud.

He reached across to snap a piece of chocolate from the bar she held and nodded. 'It's a big step—an entire lifestyle change. But I don't doubt that you're up for the challenge. You'll do a wonderful job. You'll be a wonderful mother.'

She bit her lip. 'It wasn't part of The Plan.' She'd created The Plan after her experience with

Otis, to keep her on track and make everyone proud of her—so she didn't let them down again.

'This isn't exactly the kind of thing one can plan for.'

'The thing is…' she popped another piece of chocolate into her mouth, her heart thumping '… in some ways it's *better* than The Plan.'

She stiffened. 'Not losing Tina, that's—'

She broke off, fighting the burn in her eyes and the ache in her heart. She still couldn't believe her dearest friend in the world had such a limited time left on earth. It was monumentally unfair. It made her want to yell and throw things…and cry until there weren't any tears left.

She pushed the gathering darkness away. She couldn't allow her grief for what would happen in the future to harm what time she had left with Tina. Her friend had a live-in-the-moment mantra and she'd begged Bree to follow it for the time being too.

She tried to find a smile. 'What I mean is having the opportunity to raise Tilly is an unbelievable honour.' It felt like a gift. 'I've been smitten with that kid from the day she was born.' She'd been Tina's birth partner, had taken annual leave to coincide with Tilly's birth to support Tina. 'I feel…incredibly lucky.'

Two lines appeared between Noah's eyes. 'You

make it sound like a negative, but it's a positive, isn't it?'

She tried to appear casual when everything inside her clamoured and panicked—the exact opposite of the calm control she'd been trying to cultivate since she was nineteen years old. 'It's just…if having the opportunity to raise Tilly is so much better than anything on The Plan, what else on it is…lacking?'

'So change The Plan.'

He said it as if it were the simplest thing in the world, and for the first time it occurred to her that maybe it was.

'Obviously,' she started slowly, 'I've already had to change it.'

'To include Tilly.'

In that moment it occurred to her what a great uncle he'd make. With his patience, good heart and easy humour. One day he'd make a great dad too.

The thought made her mouth dry, though she couldn't explain why.

She tried to get her mind back on track and focus on the here and now. She cleared her throat. 'So I'm now thinking maybe I don't want to open my own clinic either.'

The words felt odd to say after she'd been saying them for the best part of seven years, but they also felt freeing. As long as she could create a new plan—and stick to it—changing the old plan wouldn't send her careening off the rails or turn her into a reckless ninny.

Not if she was careful.

Noah had started to bite into an apple, but he halted—mouth open, teeth touching the skin, but yet to break it. He lowered the apple still intact. 'What…never?'

'Never say never, I guess,' she said, testing the freedom of a more flexible approach to plan making…and liking it. 'But not in the foreseeable future. I saw all the hours you and Ryder worked in the early days to get Fitness Ark up and running, the commitment it demanded of you.'

'Ask either one of us and we'd tell you it was worth every second.'

She nodded. They deserved their success and she was happy for them. 'For the next few years, though, I want to focus on creating a stable home for Tilly. And to be brutally honest, Noah,' she added quickly to forestall him from telling her that was an admirable goal, 'I'm not feeling the tiniest bit disappointed or wistful about not being my own boss.'

He finally bit into the apple, took his time chewing and swallowing, as if he was considering the things she'd just confided to him with that same slow deliberation. One of the things she'd always loved about Noah was the way he thought before he spoke.

She blinked. Loved? Loved in a completely platonic 'he's been my friend forever' kind of way. That was what she meant. *Of course.*

'If you want to run your own business, you have to want it really badly.'

She nodded.

'If you don't want it with a passion…'

'Then I shouldn't do it,' she finished for him. 'Which is why I have to come up with another plan.'

His face suddenly cleared. 'That's the reason for the road trip! To give you time to sort through all of this stuff—the wide open road as a metaphor for all of the possibilities at your feet.'

'Ha! Mrs Miller's English classes weren't lost on you after all.'

He grinned. 'Everyone loves a good metaphor.'

'I knew a road trip would force me to slow down.'

The smile slid from his face. 'I've messed that up for you.'

She shook her head. 'Having you along, our conversations, has made me realise something important. I don't have to replace the original plan with one equally rigid. I've been so focussed on the absolute right way to move forward that I'd developed a kind of blinkered vision.'

He didn't look as if he believed her.

'In the same way your plan to marry Courtney was blinkered.' She hoped it didn't upset him, her mentioning it. 'You can see now what a mistake it would've been—that it wouldn't have made either of you happy in the long term. And I'm starting to see the same with me and The Plan.'

His gaze abruptly turned from hers to stare out over the river. *Damn.* She had upset him.

She tried for levity. 'I'm breaking up with The Plan.'

He didn't crack so much as a smile.

'Noah, our conversations have made me realise that it's crazy to try and map out our entire futures. There are always going to be things we can't plan for.' If she could focus on just doing two things right—being a good parent to Tilly, and finding work that would satisfy her…oh, and keeping all reckless impulses under wraps—then maybe that would be enough. Maybe she could define that as success?

The rigid line of his jaw lost the worst of its hardness. 'That's true.'

'There are some non-negotiables, obviously. I'll need a home for Tilly and I to live. That means swapping apartment living for a place in the suburbs with a yard and that's close to good schools. I'll need a job so I can support us. Given my qualifications, though, finding a job I'll hopefully enjoy shouldn't be too difficult.'

For the first time it suddenly felt as if she could do all of this, and do it well. Without screwing any of it up.

'Bree!'

Noah seemed to light up from the inside out and it made her pulse hammer. 'What?'

'Then this is the perfect time for you to join Ryder and me at Fitness Ark. You'd be able to lay the groundwork for both the physio and dietician side of things before Tilly comes to live with you. When she does, we have a crèche at the gym, which would give you inbuilt childcare.' His lips thinned. 'Plus your job would be secure. The Frasers can't touch us.'

It sounded perfect. Utterly perfect. She'd love to be the person to expand that side of Fitness Ark's operations. Not only would she love the work and the variety it promised, but she'd never find a comparable job that would suit her half so well in a practical sense. But it was impossible.

A big black cloud loomed over her future and, no matter how hard she tried to shift it, it refused to budge. She needed to find a way to embrace it.

It won't be so bad, she told herself for the hundredth time. She forced a smile to suddenly uncooperative lips. 'Except for one small tiny thing,' she made herself say.

'What's that?'

'I'm planning to move to Hobart.' She shrugged, forced a laugh. 'So the commute would be a killer.'

He stared at her as if he hadn't heard her properly, as if her words made no sense. 'Moving to Hobart?'

'Relocating,' she said, leaving no room for misinterpretation.

He tossed his apple core into the river. 'Your entire family is in Brisbane, Bree. Your family is going to be your support network. Your parents will want to be grandparents to Tilly, while your brothers will want to be hands-on uncles.'

'And you?' she found herself asking.

He nodded. 'And me too.'

She knew exactly everything she was leaving behind, and she mourned it already. A weight pressed down on her, but she kept her chin high and refused to let her shoulders sag. 'But…you can all come to visit.' She hated how small her voice sounded. 'You will, won't you?'

'Of course we will. But why leave at all? In all likelihood Tilly won't be at school yet and—'

He broke off and she saw the exact moment he realised.

'Tina's parents,' he murmured.

'They're losing their daughter, Noah. I can't take Tilly away from them as well.'

* * *

Two days later they arrived in Melbourne, and were settled in a neat and tidy serviced apartment on the South Bank that enjoyed comprehensive views of the Yarra River.

Bree returned to the apartment after a day of browsing the shops, and wondered how Noah had filled his day. Closing the door with her hip, she set her various parcels to the floor—most of them gifts for Tina and Tilly—and pulled an envelope from her handbag.

She frowned, tapping it against her fingers as she waited for the kettle to boil. What on earth had she been thinking? It was totally inappropriate and—

'What you got there?'

Noah emerged from his bedroom, making her jump.

Worn jeans were slung low on lean hips and a navy T-shirt plastered itself to his chest. With his hair tousled and a faint shadow darkening his jaw he looked like every woman's vision of the ultimate dreamboat. Yearning rose through her hot and hard, her tongue snaking out to moisten arid lips. He followed the action, his gaze darkening.

They both looked away at the same moment.

Dear God. 'Oh, nothing.' She slid the envelope into the back pocket of her jeans before grabbing coffee mugs from the cupboard, but her assumed nonchalance failed when she realised she'd missed her pocket and the envelope fell to the floor instead, landing at Noah's feet.

Pouncing on it would be too revealing. All she could hope was that he'd hand it back without reading the logo stamped on the front.

His brows shot up the moment he leaned down to pick it up.

No such luck, then.

He pointed to the logo. 'Doesn't look like nothing to me.'

She blew out a breath when he handed it back to her. 'On the spur of the moment I got us tickets to tomorrow's game.'

Two of the Australian Football League's most iconic clubs were meeting for what was expected to be one of the clashes of the season at the MCG.

Noah's entire face lit up.

She'd so wanted to give him a treat to thank him for being so supportive about Tina and Tilly. She'd wanted to find something that would help chase away the shadows that lingered in his eyes.

So he'd made a mistake where Courtney was concerned. She knew what it felt like to make a mistake. He needed to stop beating himself up about it.

She bit back a sigh. 'But, of course, it was a stupid thing to do and a waste of money.' She'd bought the tickets on impulse, without considering the wider implications—but she didn't have to compound her mistake as she had in Sydney.

'What do you mean? We're not setting off on the *Spirit of Tasmania*—' the overnight ferry that would take them from Port Melbourne to Devonport in Tasmania '—until Monday night. There'll be plenty of time to watch tomorrow's game. We'll have all of Monday to pack and do any last-minute shopping.'

'Time isn't the problem, Noah. This is going to be one of the biggest games of the year. There's going to be a lot of media interest in the game. Which means the likelihood of you being recognised is disproportionately high.' Especially after what had happened in Sydney.

But… 'You can go!' She shoved the tickets at him. 'It won't matter if you get photographed alone.' He could still enjoy the treat.

His stance widened. 'We can both go.'

'I'm sorry, Noah, but I really couldn't bear any more speculation about our relationship in the papers. Tina and her parents must be having kittens already and—'

'Are you worried about their reactions to the Sydney fiasco?'

'Yes. No.' She pushed her hair off her face. 'Not really. I know they'll understand, but—'

'The timing has been less than ideal.'

She stabbed a finger at him. 'Don't even start

thinking this is your fault. I just…' She pressed her hands together. 'I just don't want to give them anything else to worry about. They have enough to deal with already.'

He turned thoughtful, moved her gently aside. 'Tea or coffee?'

'Tea, please.'

He made the tea and they sat on the sofas that rested at right angles to each other. They'd each claimed a sofa of their own when they'd first walked into the apartment. He eyed her over the rim of his mug. 'What if I could guarantee that we wouldn't be recognised?'

'If you could guarantee that then I'd be there like a shot, but you can't.'

'Oh, ye of little faith, Bree. I can and I will.'

Noah spun on the chair and spread his arms wide. 'What do you think?'

Bree's jaw dropped, making him laugh.

'I'd have walked past you on the street and not even recognised you. And I've known you for-ever. Ahmed, you're a genius!'

Noah had met Ahmed at university, and, al-though Ahmed had switched from computer engineering to cinematography in their second year, they'd remained friends.

Ahmed was now working for a TV production company in Melbourne doing everything from make-up and special effects to film editing. All it had taken was a phone call from Noah explaining what he needed, and Ahmed had been immediately on board with creating believable disguises for Bree and Noah.

'Given everything that's happened over the last week, I figured it was time you copped a break, Noah.'

Had it only been a week ago that Courtney had left him standing at the altar like a fool?

One week and one day.

It felt as if his entire worldview had changed in the course of those eight days.

He snapped back when Bree moved across and bent down to peer into his face. She wore a dark wig in a shaggy Suzi Quatro style, and the make-up Ahmed's assistant had chosen completely changed her skin tone. Rather than her usual tropical tan she now had a pale nearly white, slightly pasty complexion. But he'd have still recognised her. Those melt-in-your-mouth milk-chocolate eyes were exactly the same.

Ahmed surveyed her and nodded his satisfaction. 'You are still pretty, but no longer so glamorously beautiful.'

She blinked and straightened, and Noah could breathe again.

'Glamorous? Me?' She laughed. 'You didn't tell me your friend was such a charmer, Noah.'

Something inside him stilled. Glamorous wasn't the word he'd have used to describe Bree, but maybe that was just because he'd known her for so long.

It was an undeniable fact, though, that Bree Allenby was a very beautiful woman. And he wanted her. With the kind of fierce desire that pumped an urgent heat through his blood and had his every sense drinking in the sight, sound and scent of her.

He wanted to add taste and touch to that profusion of sense sensation too—craved them.

Which meant he was going to hell.

He clenched his hands. He'd never *act* on those impulses. It was out of the question. He needed to exorcise all such thoughts from his mind.

He could've groaned out loud when she bent down to peer into his face once more. 'Even the colour of your eyes has changed.'

'Brown contact lenses,' Ahmed said.

'And you've given him a full bushranger beard. It's amazing how that one thing changes everything else.'

It had taken a long time to apply—a lot of hair and glue had been involved. He'd been ordered to not scratch his face. Which meant he now itched all over.

'It hides the shape of his jaw and chin...makes him look less clean-cut.'

He'd been careful to cultivate a clean-cut wholesomeness as a teenager in an effort to distance himself from his parents. They'd never taken any real interest in their appearance—other than to look like the kind of people you didn't want to mess with.

His gut tightened. Did he look like his father?

He reached up and stroked his beard. Bree's smile nearly slayed him.

'You look great. Talk about fun!'

In that moment he didn't care what he looked like. All he cared about was making sure she enjoyed herself at today's game.

'At least the shape of your mouth is the same.'

He ground his back molars together. *Don't think about mouths or lips or what the hell mouths and lips can do or—*

'Right.' Ahmed clapped his hands. 'Time for your new outfits. At the moment you both look far too put-together.'

'This man is so good for my ego.' Bree winked at Noah before striding off with Ahmed's assistant.

He watched her go, things inside him clenching and softening. How could a woman create such conflicting sensations in him? It was just… her ego shouldn't need boosting.

Why had he never realised how deeply her experience with Otis had affected her or how widespread those effects had been? Or that she continued to punish herself for that one youthful mistake? She was starting to forgive herself, though, was learning to trust herself again. No longer being so rigid about The Plan was proof of that.

Otis was losing his hold on her. Noah would do all he could to speed up the process. And he also planned to try and change his own focus as she'd urged him to—to concentrate on the positives and the future, rather than on the negatives and the past.

'C'mon, Noah, let's make you thoroughly unrecognisable.'

Twenty minutes later, Noah couldn't hold back a bark of laughter when he and Bree stood side by side and stared at their reflections in the floor-length mirror. They both wore football jerseys, and Bree had a beanie pulled down low over her ears. Her jersey and beanie clashed with the sparkly purple high-top sneakers she wore. It was an outfit she'd normally never be caught dead in.

Speaking of not being caught dead in an outfit, though… The tail of his flannelette shirt hung out beneath his jersey and over the top of his baggy jeans. He looked scruffy and unkempt. No one who knew him would *ever* recognise him.

She grinned at him like a little kid playing

dress-ups. 'This was an inspired idea, Noah. I so have to take a photo of us.' Bree fished out her phone. 'They'll never believe this back home.'

Home. A weight pressed down on him. It wouldn't feel like home if Bree weren't there. Did she really have to relocate to Hobart?

Instinct told him that while her heart was wholly committed to Tilly and providing the very best life she could for the little girl—and he admired her more than he could say for that—she was less overjoyed at the prospect of relocating to the country's southernmost state.

Or was he simply projecting his own feelings onto her?

'Okay, we need pseudonyms to complete the charade.'

Bree's voice broke into his thoughts.

'Something starting with an N for you. If I start to say "Noah" I'll be able to turn it into…' she reached up and tapped his beard '… Ned!'

He laughed at her overt reference to one of Australia's most notorious bushrangers. 'Fine, if I'm Ned then you're Bonnie.'

'Oh! Now I want to call you Clyde.'

'No, no,' Ahmed remonstrated. 'Don't forget the name of the game is to blend in and be as invisible as possible. Not to draw attention to yourselves. You are Ned and Bonnie, die-hard football fans from the western suburbs—Lilydale, if anyone should ask. You drink beer or soda, not wine, and you eat pies and hotdogs, not caviar.'

Bree nodded once. 'Got it.'

Her eyes sparkled and Noah couldn't help but be infected by her enthusiasm. He glanced at his watch. They'd have to make a move. 'I can't thank you enough for this, Ahmed.'

'I was glad to help. Now go and enjoy yourselves.'

The ground was crowded when they got there even though there was still an hour to go till game time. And not a single soul gave them so much as a second look.

No, that wasn't entirely true. There'd been a tense moment when they'd lined up to buy their lunch—pies and sodas as instructed by Ahmed—when the guy in front had turned and halted for a moment, his brow furrowing as he stared at Noah.

'Jacko? From Gallagher's Autos?'

Noah had been careful to keep his answer short and on point. 'Ned. Lilydale. Plumber.'

'Sorry, mate, wrong bloke.'

With a clap to Noah's shoulder he'd sauntered off with his beer. Bree—Bonnie—had buried her face in the back of Ned's shoulder to suppress her laughter. He'd had to suppress an urge to swing around and high-five her.

They found their seats and ate their food, and as the stadium filled up around them the air of expectation and excitement filled them both.

'There has to be at least fifty thousand people here,' she said.

He glanced around. 'Probably closer to sixty.' And not a soul recognised them. They could relax their guard and focus on the moment, and have fun. 'This was the best idea, Br—Bonnie. Thanks for getting tickets.'

She shrugged. 'I wanted to thank you for being so supportive. Besides, you deserve to let your hair down and have some fun.'

Those eyes could slay a guy when they looked at him like that. The thing was, he'd had fun—road-tripping with her. When he should've been cast down in the doldrums, he'd instead been rediscovering his love for life and adventure.

While Bree had used The Plan to keep herself on too tight a leash, he'd been holding himself back in a similar fashion in an attempt to mould and shape his life into something it wasn't. Or would ever be. He was starting to realise that what he'd thought would make him happy was nothing more than an empty promise.

His past didn't belong in the here and now; he had nothing to prove to anyone, least of all himself. The fact he could never attain that imagined level of perfection didn't leave him feeling like a failure any more either.

That was why he'd been determined to make today happen for Bree. The expression on her face when she'd realised the likelihood of them being recognised would prevent them from attending the game had speared through the centre of him. He'd wanted to make things right for her.

'N-Ned?'

He thumped back to the present. 'You couldn't have come up with a better treat.'

Her smile widened and it occurred to him that a large portion of her enjoyment was due to his enjoyment. It had all the hard places inside him softening.

When the game started, though, she couldn't hide either her enjoyment or her enthusiasm. She yelled and cheered as loud as anybody. The game was end-to-end stuff and everything it had been hyped up to be.

At half-time their team was up by only two points after having lost some ground in the second quarter. 'I'm not going to be able to put up with that tension for another half!' But her grin belied her words.

'I'm going to be hoarse by the time we're done,' he agreed.

They launched into a blow-by-blow discussion of the half. As the little sister of two sports-mad brothers, Bree could hold her own in any sporting match post-mortem. They were concentrating so hard on their conversation it wasn't until nearby cheers and friendly jostling from the crowd roused them. A neighbouring fan pointed at the big screen and Noah wanted to groan out loud. Kiss cam! How the hell had a bloody camera picked them out of a crowd this size for the ridiculous pastime of—?

His thoughts screamed to a halt when Bree seized his face in her hands and slammed her lips to his. He was too shocked to move, though his hands did go to her shoulders to steady her.

Dear God. His eyes fluttered closed. Her lips were warm and soft and eminently kissable.

Don't move.

Don't kiss her back.

Don't do anything.

Did he imagine it or did her lips cling for a moment longer than necessary?

And then she was back in her seat and cheers sounded all around them and the camera moved on to some other poor victims.

Not that he felt like a victim. He felt *electrified.*

'Sorry,' she murmured so only he could hear. 'I thought the less time the cameras were on us, the better.'

'Good thinking. It was a smart move… Bonnie.'

His use of her pseudonym made her smile, lightening things between them again, but underneath ran a new raw thread of tension and nothing he did could shift it.

The second half of the game was just as exciting as the first, but he couldn't shake his awareness of the woman beside him. Still, when the game went to the wire and their team won it with a goal in the dying seconds, they went as mad as everyone in the stands around them.

She threw her arms around his neck with a whoop of elation.

He lifted her off her feet, even though there was no room to swing her around.

She eased back. Their eyes met. She stilled, her smile slipping. He released her, letting the full length of her body slide down his. It sent a hot hungry surge of desire Mexican-waving through his blood. When her feet finally touched the ground she stepped away, instantly ducking her head to tuck the hair of her wig back behind her ears and readjusting her beanie.

Get a grip!

'Best game ever!' he said, putting on his finest game face.

Her answering grin was his reward. 'At the end I wanted to win so bad I don't know how I'd have coped with losing. Seeing a game live is so different from watching it on the telly.'

They exited the stadium and the crowd thinned as he and Bree walked through the park, back towards their apartment. Their chatter petered out as if neither could maintain the pretence once they were away from the stadium full of people. They found themselves alone in the still night with the city lights shining like a promise in front of them.

Was he imagining her tension? Maybe she sensed the growing tension in him. Maybe he was infecting her with tension!

He searched his mind for a topic of conversation that would keep things light, keep things bearable until they reached the apartment and he could imprison himself in the sanctuary of his bedroom. *Alone.*

'Noah, about that kiss.' She swung to him as they strode across a little bridge that arced over a tiny tributary of the river, the water in it reflecting the city lights. 'I know I took you off guard and probably shocked you and weirded you out and stuff. In hindsight I shouldn't have done it. I should've done what you were doing and just faced them down, but I panicked and—'

'I wasn't weirded out, Bree.'

Her eyes looked huge in the moonlight. 'You weren't?'

Her voice sounded small and a little forlorn

and it caught at him. 'The thing is, Bree, what I really wanted to do was kiss you back.'

Her eyes grew even bigger and rounder. But the expression in them was neither shocked nor appalled.

His hand went either side of her on the railing, and he couldn't find it in him to regret his honesty. 'What I really want to do is kiss you now.'

CHAPTER SEVEN

NOAH WANTED TO kiss her!

Bree's heart leapt into her throat and pounded so hard and fast she could barely catch her breath.

In the half dark, wearing that full beard and those unfamiliar clothes, he looked both familiar and unfamiliar. With her own long dark locks and high-top sneakers, she felt like someone different, someone who...

She tossed her hair and lifted her chin. 'Kiss cam replay...' She pulled in a breath and assumed a sports commentator's voice. 'We've been treated to an extraordinary half of football here today, folks. The crowd needs half-time and a chance to catch their breath as much as the players do. And what a magnificent crowd we have in here today. Let's take a look and see who we can find in the crowd...'

She mimed a camera panning around the crowd.

'Now, there's a fine-looking couple—Ned and

Bonnie—completely decked out in their team's colours. They have to be happy with the way their team has handled themselves so far. Come on, guys, pucker up for the camera…'

Noah's eyes burned like bright points in the darkness. Her heart pounded harder and faster as a crazy freedom pumped through her blood, making her want to laugh and dance and sing.

She cocked an eyebrow. 'They might need some encouragement, folks…'

She was playing with fire, but she couldn't help it. She'd kept all her impulses on such a tight leash for the last seven years and it felt as if all of them had suddenly burst free. Just for today she was Bonnie—a girl with no past and no hang-ups.

Noah-Ned stared at her, the expression in his eyes growing fiercer and more intense. She'd never seen that expression on his face before and it made him seem even more of a stranger.

'Are you daring me to kiss you?'

Her lips lifted—flirty, taunting…daring. 'C'mon, Ned…' she kept up the sports commentator's voice '…what are you…man or mouse?'

He moved in so close his warmth and his scent crowded her. Her pulse went wild.

'I'm not the kind of guy to back down from a dare like that.'

'That's what I'm counting on.' She reached up

and touched a hand to his cheek. 'I've never been kissed by a guy with a beard before.'

'Then I think it's time to rectify that oversight.'

His lips lowered to hers—not with the speed of a man intent on proving he was man rather than mouse…or with the predatory hunger of a wolf—but a man intent on enjoying every tantalising moment of the kiss in all its build-up and execution.

The realisation made things inside her clench and soften, both at the same time. As if she were toffee and he were heat and the moment their lips touched there'd be melting and melding and even more melting.

His lips hovered over hers, mere millimetres away, and she knew he was giving her the chance to change her mind and step back, but she wasn't going anywhere.

Every single part of her craved this kiss. And whatever price she might have to pay later, she'd pay it gladly.

And then the gap closed and his lips were on hers.

His lips were far gentler than she'd expected, softer and more…patient, more giving, more… *delicious*! Noah's kiss was utterly and captivatingly delicious as if it was purely designed to slowly seduce her every sense and have her clamouring for more.

And it was a lullaby of a kiss, which sounded wrong because that suggested it was sleep-inducing and that was as far from the truth as one could get. But if felt safe to let down every barrier she'd ever had and let herself be swept away by the excitement of the kiss because beneath it all it was like coming home after the longest day of your life and being welcomed with all your favourite things.

Bree wrapped her arms around Noah and held him close, opening herself up and welcoming this gift of a kiss with gratitude and something deeper—some part of herself she had yet to name—revelling in every delicious moment.

As if he'd been waiting for her full surrender, the pressure of Noah's lips increased. Not all at once, but the pressure, the depth of kiss, increased by increments until wrapping her arms around him wasn't enough. His kiss built a storm inside her, a storm that threatened to rage out of control. She pressed as close to him as she could, her hands tunnelling into his hair to drag him even nearer and she was cursing the barrier of their clothes.

Their kiss unfolded…expanded…transformed into a storm-tossed sea of need and heat and the only thing that would calm it was more…

More Noah.

His hand tunnelled beneath her shirt and the

skin-on-skin contact—his hand exploring the small of her back—had her drawing back to suck in a breath, before her mouth collided with his again. Tongues tangoed and teeth grazed kiss-plumped lips in an ever deeper dance.

It wasn't until a series of catcalls and whistles broke into the desire-hazed fog of her mind and someone shouted, 'Get a room,' that she and Noah sprang apart.

Noah not Ned. That kiss had been pure unadulterated essence of Noah.

She touched her lips. They pulsed full and sensitive beneath her fingertips, burning with a new hunger and knowledge. Like Eve and the apple, Bree should never have flirted with temptation. She shouldn't have plucked the apple or sampled the fruit. Because that fruit—Noah—was forbidden to her.

Now she knew what he tasted like. And now she would always want.

Noah stepped in front of her as a group of men—all a little drunk and wearing football scarves and beanies—thunked across the bridge, good-naturedly razzing the couple and exchanging 'Great game' comments with Noah.

Bree's cheeks burned while everything inside her continued to jostle and clash as if the hurricane of need Noah's kiss had created inside her would never be stilled again.

'Bree?'

He'd given up the pretence too. He knew it wasn't Bonnie who'd kissed him but Bree.

She'd kissed Noah!

Noah, her friend forever.

Noah, her brothers' best friend, and Ryder's business partner.

Noah, her parents' *other* son.

Bree had never considered Noah in a brotherly light. Never. But he'd always been one of her most important friends. And his importance to her family couldn't be overstated.

'Bree, are you all right?'

He bent down to peer into her face and she flinched.

He stiffened and stepped back, and absurdly then she wanted to cry.

She forced her chin up. 'I'm fine.' She couldn't do anything to damage his relationships with her family. A mistake like that would hurt everyone.

It would hurt him most of all.

She couldn't do it. She just couldn't. It would be a thousand times worse than the mistake she'd made with Otis.

This attraction was nothing more than a temporary aberration—them letting off steam because they were both under a lot of pressure. If it were anyone else, she'd see it through to its natural conclusion, but it wasn't just anyone.

She had to make sure nothing like this happened between them again. Gesturing that they should start walking, she said, 'Let's go somewhere a little more public before we talk about what just happened.'

He didn't say anything—his face had shuttered closed. Shoving his hands in his pockets, he led them towards the bright lights of the Southbank's restaurants and bars.

They found a vacant bench that looked out over the Yarra River. She sat. He remained standing until she asked him to sit too. She'd decided during the silence of their short walk that laying it out swiftly and without room for misinterpretation would be the best strategy. 'I don't want that to ever happen again, Noah.'

He gave a mirthless laugh. 'That's become pretty obvious, Bree.'

Had she hurt his feelings? She didn't want to hurt his feelings. 'We're friends, not friends with benefits. That would never work for us.'

His expression didn't change. She opened her mouth to try and temper her words. With a superhuman effort she closed it again. It was better she hurt his feelings briefly now than to cause an estrangement between him and her family.

'Noah, my life is in flux at the moment.' She stared at the light reflected on the river rather than at him. 'And I'd be lying if I said I wasn't finding that confronting.'

He angled towards her. She glanced at him briefly and shrugged. 'Tina's illness guts me. I'm honoured to be entrusted with Tilly's welfare, though, and a part of me is excited at the prospect, but that doesn't stop it feeling overwhelming and frightening. I know a part of me has been searching for distraction and comfort.'

She wished he'd say something. Agree with her. 'I don't want to use you in that way,' she whispered. 'It'd be unforgivable.'

'Not unforgivable,' he finally said. 'Understandable…human.' He glanced up at the sky and then back at her. 'But if you think a kiss like that is a common thing, you're wrong.'

She knew then she only had to say the word and he'd take her back to the apartment and they'd make love all night. Everything inside her clenched with hunger and need. He *wanted* that to happen.

She did all she could to channel common sense. 'It would change things between us, and you matter too much for me to risk that. You matter too much to my family. And we all matter too much to you.'

His glare drilled through her and she could see he thought her a coward. It stung. 'It would be a bigger mistake than the one I made with Otis.'

She thumped a hand to her chest. 'And I would hate myself for it.'

His head rocked back as if she'd slapped him.

'How on earth am I supposed to raise a child if I can't conquer such self-destructive impulses in myself? I never want to screw up on that Otis scale again.'

'What happened with Otis doesn't make you a screw-up. You were taken in by the guy—played. Hell, Bree, you were just a kid. It wasn't your fault. And in case it's escaped your notice—' his eyes flashed '—I'm not Otis.'

He wasn't, but she'd completely lost her head over Otis, and she'd let that override her judgement, had let it silence the warnings sounding through her. She'd turned a blind eye when she shouldn't have. She wasn't making those same mistakes with Noah.

Her every hormone clamoured to make love with him, but her every instinct warned her not to. She'd listen to her voice of reason rather than her bad angel, thank you very much.

'Nobody blames you for what happened back then.'

'I know.' And she did. She knew that none of her family held her responsible.

'But you blame yourself enough for everyone, right?'

His scorn made her stiffen.

'By your estimate, your judgement is far superior to everyone else's, right?'

Her mouth opened and closed but she couldn't push a single sound out.

'You can't accept that you made a mistake and move on. You have to keep punishing yourself instead.'

She thrust out her jaw. 'I'm moving on!'

'Sticking to a rigid, sterile plan isn't—' he made air quotes that infuriated her '—"moving on".'

'The Plan,' she bit out through gritted teeth, 'has become far more flexible, as you're well aware. And what's your definition of moving on anyway? Me sleeping with you will prove I've moved on? Hell, Noah, why on earth would I do that? Why would I—' it was her turn to make air quotes '—"move on" with *you*?'

He went so still it almost frightened her. She did what she could to get her voice back under control. 'You—'

He shot to his feet. 'You've said enough.'

She wanted to cry because he'd taken her words the wrong way—not just the wrong way, but the worst possible way. Maybe it was for the best. She needed to kybosh any chance of anything ever happening between them.

The expression in his eyes, though, cut her to the marrow. She couldn't do it. 'Eight days ago you were going to marry Courtney Fraser. Right at this very moment you should be on your darn honeymoon! I don't think you're in any better frame of mind at the moment than I am.'

She rose too. '*That's* what I meant, Noah. So you needn't go all dark and Heathcliff on me. I didn't mean that I think I'm too good for you and I sure as hell don't think you're beneath me.'

She started to turn away, but swung back. 'And the fact you thought for a moment that I'd think such a thing tells me exactly how screwed up you currently are.'

He dragged both hands back through his hair and then nodded. 'Point taken.'

'I'm going back to the apartment.'

'I'm not.'

Good. The less time they spent together at the moment, the better. She didn't ask him what he planned to do or where he was going.

'Tomorrow?' she forced herself to ask.

'I'm busy all day.'

Again, good. But her stomach gave a sick roll all the same.

'If I decide that I'm going to Tasmania, I'll meet you on the ferry tomorrow evening.'

So…he was jumping ship?

It was for the best, she told herself. Going their separate ways was the smart thing to do. If only she could make herself feel it.

* * *

Bree boarded the *Spirit of Tasmania* and told herself it was ludicrous to feel lonely. She'd never planned to have company on the trip. *This* was how it was supposed to be.

Dumping her suitcase in her cabin, which was tiny, nothing more than two shelves holding a single mattress each, a bench masquerading as a desk, and a tiny en suite bathroom.

'They never promised five stars,' she reminded herself, and then went out to explore the upper decks.

There was a variety of cafés, restaurants and bars, lounge areas to watch the big-screen TVs. She ventured outside when they cast off, but it was ridiculously windy so she hastened back inside.

She had a whole evening ahead of her—nothing scheduled, no pressure…nothing. She should be glad of it, should be enjoying the downtime. Instead of a blank canvas of possibility, though, it just felt blank and boring and as dull as the dark night outside the ferry's windows.

Treating herself to a glass of Shiraz, she retreated to a table for two by a window. Not that there was anything to see. The window merely reflected the room inside back at her. When she met the eyes of a bearded man in them it took her a moment to realise who she was looking at.

Noah.

She schooled herself to turn slowly to face him. His lips lifted and so did his eyebrows. He gestured to the other chair at her table. He was a good eight feet away, but relief made her shoulders sag. She smiled and nodded back.

He sat with alacrity…and purpose. 'I owe you an apology. I acted like a jackass last night. I don't know what came over me.'

Relief flooded her, unbending her whole body. 'Yesterday was a crazy day. The Ned and Bonnie disguises, the euphoria of the game—' *that kiss* '—it's been a crazy week, Noah.'

The craziest damn week of his life, that was for sure.

Noah worked at making things right between him and Bree again, worked at making her feel good about herself and not blame herself for *anything*. That was why he was here, why he'd shown up.

Last night he'd gone to the casino, had played a few games of Blackjack before wandering the streets of inner-city Melbourne, trying to dampen the flame that kissing Bree had ignited inside him.

She was right—just over a week ago he'd been

about to marry Courtney. He had no business kissing anyone.

He found himself resenting Courtney. Not for making a laughing stock of him when she'd walked out of their wedding ceremony—he'd deserved that. Not for hiding her fears from him and refusing to discuss them with him until it was too late.

He found himself resenting her for having distracted him from what had been right under his nose these last two years—*Bree*! And that made no sense at all. He'd never considered Bree in those terms, and he didn't want to start now.

Bree was off limits.

He'd never thought of her as a sister or anything like that, but he owed the Allenbys everything. If Janice and Colin hadn't taken him under their wings he shuddered to think what would've become of him. He'd rather cut his own arm off than hurt them. Which meant a temporary hookup with Bree was out of the question.

If he could only get the thought of it out of his mind.

If only that kiss hadn't blown his world apart.

He'd kissed a few women in his time, but no kiss had touched him the way Bree's kiss had. Maybe she was right. Maybe that kiss had been nothing more than a pressure valve helping them to release all of their pent-up tension.

But it had felt like more.

'You're on the hard stuff, I see?' Bree gestured to his can of soda.

He dragged himself back to the present. 'I figure my liver needs a rest after Coffs Harbour.'

She grinned, but an element of wariness remained in the depths of her brown eyes and at the edges of her smile. He needed to dispel that unease...and mistrust?

The thought she might no longer trust him was a physical pain. 'Bree, I promise what happened last night won't happen again. You're right, emotions have been running high this trip and I had no right to...'

Those brown eyes widened. He swallowed. He *wouldn't* kiss her. 'No right to try and find that kind of solace with you. You mean a lot to me. If I were to lose your friendship—'

'Not going to happen!'

The sharpness of her tone and the way she straightened eased some of the burning in his gut.

'And I'm sorry too. I shouldn't have...' she waved her hands between them '...either.'

Did she want to talk about it further? He sure as hell didn't, but he'd do whatever she wanted and needed.

'Let's draw a veil over last night. I think it'd be best if we never mentioned it again.'

'A line in the sand?' he said.

'A cone of silence.'

And then they were both laughing and her wariness slipped away, just leaving behind his buddy Bree. She gestured to his beard. 'How long are you going to keep it?'

'Ahmed said I'd get a few days out of it if I were careful, but I think I'll lose it tomorrow.'

She sipped her wine. He ran a hand down his beard. Did she like it? Was that why she'd kissed him—because he'd looked like a stranger rather than himself? Should he grow a beard for real?

'What's your plan when we hit Tassie, Noah?'

'I have a couple of days in Hobart before I head off on a week-long wilderness trek.'

Her eyes brightened. 'Really?'

'It was a great idea. Thank you.'

He went on to describe the ancient forests, mountain ranges, and river courses he hoped to see on the South West National Park trek he'd booked and that culminated in Port Davey, one of the most unique marine reserves on the planet. He was careful to keep things light and easy. Normal. Comradely.

Half an hour later he let out a long breath. For the time being he'd mended things between them. Bree wasn't staring at him as if he were a monster or someone she couldn't trust. If only he could make himself feel that same way—relaxed and at ease. But he still wanted to kiss her.

If he was brutally honest, he ached to do *much* more than kiss her and he didn't know how to rid himself of that all-consuming need.

He ground his back molars together. This whole attraction thing would fade. A week hiking up mountains and through virgin forest would help rid him of the wash of hormones that had built inside him.

Focus on making things right with her. That was what he needed to do. It was what he *would* do, regardless of how much the craving and heat buffeted him. He'd have a cold shower when he returned to his cabin. That'd help him put it all on ice.

Bree glanced past him and her gaze sharpened. 'Just give me a second.'

She made her way across to a woman huddled in a nearby armchair. Who…? Was she crying?

He was on his feet the second his suspicion was confirmed and at Bree's side.

The woman sent him a watery smile, before turning back to Bree. 'So the mix-up means there are four of us in a two-berth cabin. The kids are tired and grumpy…they both get motion sickness. And I already feel like I've not slept for a week.' She pushed her hair off her face. 'The ferry is full so they can't provide us with either a four-person cabin or an additional room.'

She waved a hand at them and shook her head. 'It was kind of you to come over, but I'll be fine. I just needed half an hour to myself. I'll need to go back soon. My husband is as worn out as I am, though he's trying to hide it…' She trailed off with a tired smile and a shrug.

Two adults and two children in one of those two-berth cabins? What a nightmare. 'I don't have a four-berth cabin to swap with you, but I can give you my two-berth cabin. Maybe you and your husband can divide and conquer and take a cabin and a kid each?'

The woman sagged as if such unexpected kindness had robbed her of speech, but it was the expression in Bree's eyes—their warmth and admiration—and the softness of her smile that made him feel like a million bucks.

'I couldn't possibly impose like that and—'

''Course you can,' Bree said. 'Noah can bunk in with me.'

'You're friends?'

'Have been for ever,' she continued in that breezy nonchalant fashion she had. 'It'll be like the old days when we used to pitch a tent in the backyard.'

Except Ryder and Blake had always been there too.

'It makes absolutely no difference to us,' Bree continued.

Bunk in with Bree? Bad idea. Super bad idea.

'Oh, I can't thank you enough! If you're sure…?'

He couldn't refuse. Her look of relief, as if a major weight had just been lifted off her, skewered him. 'Positive.' He injected every ounce of enthusiasm into that single word that he could.

In no time at all, his suitcase was in Bree's cabin—her tiny, tiny cabin—and he'd handed his room key to a very grateful Mrs Baker.

'That was a lovely thing to do,' Bree said when they sat down in the restaurant a short time later. 'The poor woman has been worn to a frazzle. They've travelled down from Newcastle with a five-year-old son and three-year-old daughter to attend a cousin's wedding in Launceston. They're obviously trying to do it as cheaply as they can, but somewhere along the way there's been a mix-up with their booking.'

'Happy to help.' In truth he'd made the offer before Bree could offer the Bakers her own cabin instead. 'With my suitcase stowed safely in your room, I'm just as happy to sleep in an armchair in one of the lounges.'

'You can't do that!'

He couldn't?

He stared into wide outraged eyes and swallowed. Evidently not.

'Noah, there's a perfectly good spare bunk going begging in my cabin. Like I said, it'll be like when we were kids and we camped out in the backyard.'

Except they were no longer kids. And her brothers wouldn't be there. And when they were kids the thought of kissing her had never entered his head.

But he knew what she was doing—she was trying to get things back to normal between them. She was trying to re-establish old boundaries. Boundaries that had been kicked to smithereens when they'd kissed.

If he wanted to prove to her that things between them were okay, he'd have to go along with this plan of hers without making a big deal out of it. 'Well, if you're sure, that'd be great,' he found himself saying.

Did he imagine the way she swallowed then as if to bolster her nerves? Was her smile a touch too bright? Did she forgo another glass of wine because she wanted to maintain her guard? Or because she didn't trust herself?

Don't!

His hand tightened around his glass of soda. *Don't even go there.* Because even if the answer to any or all of those questions was in the affirmative, it didn't change anything. He'd give her absolutely no cause for concern about anything tonight. He'd refuse to think of Bree in any way other than as a good buddy who he'd known for most of his life.

He most certainly wouldn't think about kissing her, remember how she'd felt in his arms, or recall the soft breathy sounds that had escaped the back of her throat when she'd kissed him as if her entire world had depended on it.

His fingers started to ache. With a concerted effort, he relaxed them. 'It'll be an early start in the morning. Apparently we're due to arrive in Devonport at six a.m.' If he played things right he'd spend no more than a few hours in her cabin. If he didn't go in until midnight or a bit later… and then got up at five…

That was five hours.

Five hours was nothing.

She'd be asleep.

He gritted his teeth. He could do this.

Noah glanced at the clock embedded in the shelf between the two bunks. *Two a.m.* Who knew two hours could crawl by so slowly?

The shallowness of Bree's breathing told him she was awake as well. He was tempted to ask her if his being here was bothering her, but that felt as if it would be breaking some unspoken pact and prove that things were different between them now.

He clenched his hands in the sheets. If it was the last thing he did, he'd make things right between them again. 'You awake?'

The briefest of hesitations and then, 'Uh-huh.'

'I was thinking about the Bakers and their two vomiting children,' he said. 'I expect they're having a rough night of it even though our passage has been pretty smooth so far.' Bass Strait could get notoriously rough and choppy.

'But their night will still be so much easier thanks to you.'

Her voice sounded soft in the darkness, and he couldn't explain why but it melted some of the tension that had him wound up tight. 'Bree, you said you were excited but also terrified about raising Tilly. What scares you?'

He heard her roll to her side to face him. 'Lots of things. Her heart is going to be broken when Tina dies. How do I explain it to her? How do I help her through it? How do I make it up to her?'

His stomach clenched. She was taking on so much.

She released a long breath. 'The short answer is I can't make it up to her. I just hold her when she cries, tell her it's okay to be sad, and try to make sure we do some fun things too. I guess I just surround her in as much love as I can and do all I can to make her feel secure.'

'You're going to be a brilliant mother to her, Bree.'

'I hope so, but… What do I do if she gets sick? I know nothing about childhood ailments. And crazy things plague me. What if she hates her first day of school? When she's a bit older I'd like her to play a team sport, but what if she doesn't want to? Do I force her or do I back down? What if she doesn't want to go to university? I know Tina would want her to and—'

'Bree.' He pushed upright. 'You're looking for trouble before it has a chance to find you.'

'I know! It's crazy.' She paused, then, 'I'm afraid of the temper tantrums that will inevitably happen when she's a hormone-ridden teenager and I won't let her do something she has her heart set on and she shouts, "You're not my real mother!" at me.'

He slid back down, staring up at the darkness, his heart burning. 'You can't take that stuff personally.'

'I know. But I dread it all the same.'

'Your mum will be a huge source of help, not to mention information.'

'I'll be relying on her a lot. I wish—'

She broke off and his heart clenched. She wished she'd have her mother near. She wished she weren't leaving her support network behind. She didn't say it out loud, but he knew her too well.

'I know it'll all work out, Noah. I know I'll get the hang of it. Plus everyone will visit and that'll help a lot too. There'll be lots of visits.'

'So many you'll get sick of them,' he promised.

'Never.' She laughed. 'Now, this is crazy o'clock in the morning. I'm going to take us through a guided meditation. Close your eyes.'

He did as she ordered, following her softly spoken instructions—tightening and then loosening different muscle groups, concentrating on his breathing until he felt himself floating away on a warm sea of well-being.

CHAPTER EIGHT

SHE WAS DOING a brilliant job, Bree congratulated herself the next morning. At this rate she and Noah would be back to normal and firmly in the friends' zone again in no time at all. And they'd have forgotten all about Sunday night's kiss.

Except she'd never had to work so hard before to keep things *normal* between her and Noah. Or to think of him as a friend rather than a very adult, very hot male… To not notice the broad strength of his shoulders or the depth of his chest or the lean strength of hips she recalled pressed hard against her own and…

Stop it!

Try harder.

Noah was trying his absolute best too. She couldn't fault him or blame him for not cooperating. Since driving off the ferry at a ridiculously early hour, they'd grabbed takeaway coffees from a fast-food chain's drive-through, they'd played along to a trivia quiz on morning radio, which between them they'd managed to get every question right. Actually, that had been fun.

But of a three-hour, twenty-minute trip, they still had an hour forty to go.

She launched into a description of the chocolaterie she'd had lunch at the previous day. With an entire day to kill, she'd driven out to the Yarra Valley where she'd stared at vineyards and tried to stop thinking about Noah. It hadn't worked. Nor had sampling the chocolate at the chocolaterie. But at least it gave her something to talk about now.

Eventually, though, her story petered out. She moistened her lips. 'What did you get up to yesterday? Anything fun?'

'I had lunch with Ahmed—took back the gear we borrowed—and met his new girlfriend, Susie.'

'Nice.'

A silence stretched. And stretched. Right. Let's abandon further conversation for the foreseeable future.

She was about to ask him to choose a playlist from the assortment on her phone when he said, 'I rang Courtney.'

Whoa, what? *Why?*

She glanced at him, very briefly. 'How did that go?' And then she frowned. 'She actually answered? She took your call?'

He laughed, but it lacked any real humour. 'Yeah, I wondered if she would too.'

Why had he rung her?

Before this road trip, before she'd noticed how damn hot he was and had discovered that his kiss could set her on fire and make her forget *everything*, she'd have simply asked him. But now it felt impossibly intrusive.

From the corner of her eye she saw him glance across at her. He gave a low chuckle that raised all the fine hairs on her arms. 'I can see you wrestling over there with yourself, Busy Bree.'

The old nickname had her blowing out a breath. 'I don't want to ask anything that'll make you feel awkward.' She flexed her fingers on the steering wheel. 'But I'm guessing if you didn't want to talk about it you'd have not raised the topic.'

'You can ask me anything you want.'

That sounded *too* inviting. It had things inside her burning and clamouring. It had questions like *Do you want to kiss me again?* hovering on the tip of her tongue.

She bit her tongue. Hard.

'Let me guess.' She made herself laugh, rather credibly, she thought. 'I can ask you anything, but you reserve the right not to answer?' She'd expected him to laugh too. She *wanted* him to laugh.

But he didn't. He'd gone serious.

Her fingers clenched the steering wheel. 'Why did you ring Courtney?'

He took his time answering. 'A few reasons. I wanted to make sure she was okay.'

Because he was a good guy. 'And is she?'

'She wasn't sounding particularly chipper, but she said she was fine. I wanted to apologise to her.'

She schooled her features. 'For?'

'For not being more understanding when she called the wedding off. And for...'

Her mouth went dry.

'She accused me of seeing her as a trophy, and in some respects she was right. Courtney's family come from old money so I knew she didn't want me for *my* money.'

Both Ryder and Noah had experienced money-hungry girlfriends in the past few years, since they'd become successful. It had made both of them gun-shy.

'I'd had this idea in my head of what my life would look like when I'd finally made it. For me success translated into making my life the exact opposite of my parents'.'

His parents had given him no love, no support. They'd never wanted children, and his mother had acted as if Noah were to blame for the upheaval a young child had created in her life. Rather than casting the blame where it belonged—with her and her husband's irresponsibility. They'd seemed to blame him, not only for his very existence, but their own shortcomings. She'd never understood why they'd not given him up for adoption or surrendered him into foster care.

She'd once asked him and the answer had sickened her. He'd said they only kept him for the welfare money they received. They were truly awful people and he'd deserved so much better.

'Courtney's family is the polar opposite of mine.'

She could see how his vision of the Fraser family had seduced him. For a start they actually treated each other with respect. And they'd treated Noah with respect too.

'Courtney is smart, beautiful and accomplished.'

And cold, she wanted to say but didn't.

'She knows all of the right people, moves in all the best circles. It's shallow, but it all went to my head.'

'Not shallow,' she countered. 'Understandable.' The Frasers lived an unbelievably privileged and aspirational lifestyle.

His lips tightened. 'I realise now that my wanting to marry her was an attempt to erase the past. That wasn't fair of me. I needed to apologise.'

She couldn't imagine Courtney being over-joyed to hear such a confession, though.

She glanced at him again. 'Do you still want that kind of perfect life?'

One achingly broad shoulder lifted. 'We all have a vision of a perfect future, don't we?'

'I guess.' Her perfect future involved not letting her family down again.

'But I now know that it's less to do with externals and more to do with principles…like honesty, honour, integrity. I'll never use a person again like I did Courtney, to try and make me feel good about myself. You were right, Bree. I should be proud of what I've achieved rather than ashamed of something I had absolutely no control over—like my childhood.'

His now clean-shaven jaw was thrust out. 'I've given my parents and their attitudes far too much weight in my life, but no more. I'm through with that.'

She wanted to hug him. A *friendly* hug. 'I'm glad you're finally moving on. You deserve better than to let it hold you back.' She flashed him a smile. 'You deserve your perfect future.'

'So do you, Bree.'

She was going to work hard to earn all the trust that had been placed in her—Tina's belief that she could provide Tilly with a loving home, and her family's belief that she was a good person. She wouldn't let them down.

'I also told Courtney what her father had done—having you fired—and suggested she might want to ask him to reverse that decision.'

Her eyes started from her head. 'You did *what*?'

He shrugged.

Dear God, what on earth had possessed him to bring her up in that conversation? 'Please tell me you explained that awful tabloid photograph of us.'

He folded his arms, his lips twisting. 'If she claims to know me so well—and she claims she knows me better than I know myself—then when I tell her that there's absolutely nothing going on between us, she should believe me.'

There *wasn't* anything going on between them. There was absolutely no reason why hearing him say it out loud should feel like a knife to the heart. 'But she didn't believe you?'

'She told me to go to hell, that she wouldn't be asking her father to reverse any such decision, and said she never wanted to hear from me again.'

She made a face. 'So it ended well, then.'

He laughed. 'Perhaps not as well as I'd hoped.'

'Oh, Noah, it wasn't wise to bring me up in that conversation. You'd just told the poor woman you'd fallen for what she'd represented rather than who she was. And while she might've known that, hearing it would still have stung.'

'She said she'd had a lucky escape!'

'She did. You both did!'

'And you being fired isn't right, Bree. I thought Courtney had more integrity than that.'

His lips tightened. She forced herself to focus on the road. Not on his lips and certainly not on the pounding of her heart. She refused to remember how his mouth had moved on hers or how their tongues had tangled and—

Stop it!

She rattled into speech. 'The whole getting fired thing might've happened at the perfect time anyway. It might be a sign that I should relocate to Hobart now. Get settled, find a job and start becoming a more permanent fixture in Tilly's life.'

'The only thing it's a sign of is the Frasers' spite. Courtney told me she was glad to be able to hurt me through you.'

Nice.

'And then told me she'd be glad to do me any future disservice that she could think of.'

She shrugged. 'I knew there was a reason I never liked her.'

'She also told me that all the publicity from the cancelled wedding has had business booming.'

Bree went cold all over, but after a few moments she shook it off. 'She wanted to hurt you in the same way she felt hurt. You know that, don't you?'

'Maybe. One thing's for certain—I'm glad I didn't marry her.'

'Are you done with feeling guilty about her?'

He raked both hands back through his hair. 'I'm still ashamed of the way I used her…'

He hadn't meant to use her, though. It hadn't been a conscious decision.

He blew out a breath. 'But I feel as if I can now draw a line under the whole incident and move on.'

She blew out a breath too. 'Good.'

He reached across as if to squeeze her knee and everything inside her froze. He reefed his hand back. 'I, uh… I have you to thank for that.'

'Me?' she squeaked. Dear God, don't let him say anything about their kiss setting him free or making him realise all the possibilities open to him now, or…anything like that.

'For inviting me on your trip. For discussing the hard stuff with me. It's given me a chance to come to terms with everything. I'm grateful, Bree.'

Was that why he'd kissed her—because he'd been *grateful*? It took a superhuman effort to not screw up her face.

He kissed you because you dared him to, idiot.

Forget about the kiss already, Bree!

The kiss didn't matter.

Except it felt as if it were one of the most momentous things to have ever happened to her.

She shook herself. She was just getting things muddled in her mind. The things she and Tina had to discuss, *those* were the momentous things.

'Cat got your tongue?' he teased. 'You have plenty to say when it involves me and Courtney, but nothing when I say something nice to you or pay you a compliment?'

She shook her head and smiled despite herself. 'I'm honestly glad the road trip has helped you deal with this stuff, Noah. You're a great friend and I know if our situations were reversed you'd do the same for me. Your friendship is important to me.'

'To you or to your family?' he asked quietly.

She glanced over at him in surprise, before focussing on the road again.

'And are we ever going to stop for breakfast?' he added as they drove into Campbell Town—one of the small towns en route to Hobart.

'If you see a likely café, point it out.'

'There.'

She pulled over and parked the car.

They were soon ensconced inside a warm and

cosy café enjoying waffles with maple syrup and bacon. But the entire time his question burned through her. Was his friendship important to her family or to her personally?

Of course it was important to her family, that wasn't in dispute, but…

She thought about how much she'd loathed the idea of him marrying Courtney because she'd never thought the other woman would make him happy. She thought back to how freeing it had felt to talk to him about Otis. She recalled how easily she'd confided her decision to become Tilly's guardian to him—how natural that had been and how much his admiration and support had meant.

She realised then that Noah had always been the one she'd confided her secrets to first—not Ryder or Blake or her parents…and on some occasions not even Tina. Noah had always made time for her, had never trivialised her confidences or belittled them. He'd never made her feel…less.

Her phone pinged. She read the text message and then held her phone out so he could read it too. 'You're invited to lunch at Tina's today.'

'I wasn't expecting that. I don't want to intrude.'

'You won't be intruding. She'd love to see you.' Another text hit her inbox. 'And her parents have offered you their spare room for the duration of your stay.'

'They don't have to do that!'

He opened his mouth and then straightened, his lips pursing. 'Are you sure they wouldn't mind?'

'Of course they won't mind. They'd not have made the offer if they did.'

She texted back, reciting her message out loud. '"Noah would love to come to lunch. Would also love to accept the offer of the room."'

At his nod, she sent it.

She set the phone back to the table. 'Your friendship matters to me, Noah. Not just to my family. You're one of the best friends I've ever had. I'm not sure what I would do if I were to ever lose your friendship.'

The thought made the day go dark.

He reached out and covered her hand. 'Not ever going to happen, Bree.'

'They adore each other.' Noah couldn't drag his gaze from where Bree and Tilly painted 'abstract' art on a huge piece of butcher's paper in Tina's backyard. Bree had pulled a huge packet of the stuff from the back of her car when they'd first arrived.

Once lunch was over, Bree and Tilly had raced

outside with their paper and paints, as excited as if it were Christmas morning.

Tina laughed. 'I know! It's a joy to watch, though, right?'

'Right,' he echoed, because it was. But... 'How have they become such good friends? I know Bree has spent a bit of time with you over the last couple of years, but it's just the odd three-day weekend here and there. I wouldn't have thought it'd be enough to foster this sort of connection.'

'They've always had a special bond. It's as if they just get each other. But all of that has been strengthened by our twice-weekly video conferencing chats. And believe me, we can have marathon sessions.'

'Twice a week?'

'Wednesday night is Bree's bedtime-story night where she reads a book to Tilly. Tilly always looks forward to it. And we have a longer session at some point over the weekend. Of course, with you guys travelling this week we've only had a couple of quick phone chats. Tilly has been on tenterhooks waiting for Bree to arrive.'

The little girl—a precocious dark-haired three-year-old—had been glued to Bree's side from the moment they'd arrived. She'd been less than impressed with Noah, though. She continued to glare at him with dark-eyed suspicion as if afraid he might try and monopolise Bree's time and attention.

'About what happened while we were travelling, Tina…' He glanced at the other woman, who currently looked healthy and well. There was no indication whatsoever of the ticking time bomb inside her. 'That damn picture splashed in the newspapers… It wasn't what it was made out to be.'

He glanced up when Tina's parents, Don and Corinne, joined them on the back deck. They'd insisted on cleaning up after lunch and had shooed everyone outside to enjoy the sun. 'I'd hate for you or your parents to think less of Bree or think you'd made a mistake in asking her to become Tilly's guardian.'

Tina laughed. 'Relax, Noah. Bree explained what happened and then chided me because I found it funny. But, c'mon, it is kind of funny.'

He fought a reluctant grin. 'You weren't the one who had to explain it to Ryder and Blake.'

That only made her laugh harder. Corinne joined in. 'It reminded me of when the girls were little.' She winked at Noah. 'They used to get up to so much mischief—not naughty, just high spirits—and would create the most elaborate justifications for why they'd had to do whatever it was.'

Bree and Tina had been in and out of each other's homes on a daily basis when they'd been growing up, and the memory of their laughter and antics made him smile.

Tina's mother glanced down the backyard at Bree and Tilly. 'Do you think, if we asked nicely, the girls would let us have a paintbrush and join in?'

'I'm sure of it,' Don said, lumbering to his feet and helping his wife to hers.

'Thank you again,' Noah said, 'for putting me up for a few nights. I really appreciate it.'

'We're glad you could stay, Noah,' Corinne said. 'We're looking forward to it.'

'It is nice to see you again, Noah,' Tina said as her parents made their way down to Tilly and Bree.

'It's nice to see you too.'

'So don't take this the wrong way...'

Everything inside him clenched. He *had* caused trouble for Bree—for all of them—hadn't he? Squaring his shoulders, he met Tina's gaze directly. He'd fix whatever needed fixing. It was why he was here. 'But?'

'I was surprised you accepted my parents' offer of their spare room.'

He let out a slow breath when he realised Tina had meant it—that the tabloid articles and pictures hadn't bothered her. The relief was like a cold beer on a hot day. 'It was really kind of them to offer and initially I was going to refuse, but...'

He sat up a little higher. 'The thing is, Tina, Tilly is going to become a part of Bree's family.'

She nodded.

'Bree is a part of my family—not blood, I know, but the family of my heart. Which means Tilly is going to become a part of my family too. Tilly is going to become an honorary Allenby and Tilly's grandparents are going to become a part of that circle too. I want to get to know them. That's why I accepted the offer of their spare room. I want to get to know them because we're all going to become important in each other's lives.'

Tina's eyes filled. 'That,' she whispered, 'is the most perfect answer ever. You have no idea how much it means to me…what a comfort it is.'

He swallowed the lump that lodged in his throat. 'I'm really sorry things can't be different. I'm sorry that—'

'I know.' She reached out to squeeze his hand, forestalling the rest of his words. 'But I've told everyone that we're only allowed to focus on the here and now—no sad faces. I just want to focus on the time I have left and make the most of it.'

He nodded. They stared at the tableau in front of them, chuckling when they realised Tilly had refused to allow her grandparents to paint on her and Bree's painting, but had set them up with paintbrushes and a piece of butcher's paper of their own.

'Bree is so honoured that you've asked her to become Tilly's guardian.'

'And I feel blessed that I have a friend who loves Tilly almost as much as I do.'

They were quiet for a while, simply enjoying the gentle sunshine. Noah scrolled through his phone. 'I'm determined to win your daughter's approval before I leave on my trek.' He left the day after tomorrow.

'And how do you propose to do that?' Tina's eyes danced. 'Bree is Tilly's BFF and she won't let anyone else get in the way of that.'

'I'm going to win her over with bribery.'

He held out his phone to show her what he meant and Tina clapped her hands in delight.

'We could all make a day of it tomorrow,' he suggested.

'To tell you the truth, I'd welcome a day on my own with my parents.' She glanced at him. 'I'd be awfully grateful if you, Bree and Tilly made a day of it, though.'

He nodded. Sounded great to him.

'Go on,' Tina urged, her eyes dancing again. 'Go and win my daughter over.'

Noah couldn't remember feeling this nervous about anything in a long time. But forging a re-lationship with Tilly had become one of his highest priorities. Some time in the next eighteen months, that little girl would lose her mother. It would help her to have as many friends as possible.

And it would be important to Bree.

Tilly frowned as he drew closer. 'You can help Nanna and Poppy with their picture. You can't paint on ours.'

'Now, Tilly,' her grandmother remonstrated, 'what did we say about being bossy?'

Tilly stuck her bottom lip out in mutiny, before whirling to Bree. 'But it's our picture!'

'It is,' Bree agreed. 'But we have to be polite, remember? We have to be nice to everyone.'

'Please you can't paint on our picture thank you,' Tilly said, her eyes narrowed as she glared at Noah.

Bree's lips twitched and Noah didn't know how he managed to keep a straight face, except he knew that laughing would disgrace him in the little girl's eyes.

'But maybe Noah would like to paint a picture all his own,' Bree suggested.

Tilly's face cleared and she even deigned to select a paintbrush for him while Bree organised the paper. He thanked them both gravely. 'I want to draw a wombat and a kangaroo. What are you painting?'

'You're not allowed to look until we're finished.'

'Okay, cross my heart. I'll just concentrate on my wombat and kangaroo.'

Tilly stared at him for a moment, fiddled with the charm bracelet at her wrist…and then hustled back to Bree's side.

He hummed as he painted. When he reached the end of his song, he cleared his throat. 'Maybe I'll paint a Tasmanian devil too. And an emu.'

Tilly looked up from her painting. 'And a koala?'

He pretended to consider her suggestion. 'I don't think I'd be very good at painting a koala.'

'Why not?' the little girl demanded.

'I haven't seen one for a very long time.'

'But everyone knows what a koala looks like. Don't they, Auntie Bree?' She didn't give Bree time to answer. She swung back to Noah. 'Can I see your kangaroo?'

'Only if you promise not to laugh at it. I'm a bit rusty at this painting gig and I need lots more practice.'

Tilly promised and he held his painting up for inspection. She stared. She didn't laugh. 'Your kangaroo would be better if it was pink.'

'Pink?'

'We have lots of paper so you can practise lots and lots.'

Talk about a harsh critic! Behind Tilly's back

Bree clapped a hand over her mouth to stifle a laugh.

'You know what I need before I draw a koala? I need a research trip.'

Tilly turned to Bree. 'What's that?' she whispered.

Understanding dawned in Bree's eyes. 'I think Noah is saying he needs to go and see a real live koala.'

Tilly swung back to him, her eyes wide. Noah pulled out his phone and showed them the picture of the wildlife park he'd shared with Tina earlier. 'What do you ladies think? Would you like to go and visit koalas and kangaroos and wombats and Tasmanian devils tomorrow?'

Tilly's whole face lit up. She grabbed hold of Bree's hand and swung on it. 'Can we go, Auntie Bree? Can we?'

Bree nodded. 'I couldn't think of anything I'd rather do.'

Tilly jumped up and down and cheered. The grin Bree sent Noah slayed him where he stood. 'Do you want me to show you how to draw a koala?' Tilly said.

'Yes, please.'

That frown lowered back over her eyes. 'We can still go tomorrow…even if you learn to draw a koala today?'

'We sure can.'

She held her wrist up, displaying her bracelet. 'I get a charm every birthday. I'll get another one soon when I turn—' She broke off to glance at Bree.

Bree held up four fingers. 'Four.'

'Four,' Tilly said, swinging back to him. 'Do you like it?'

'Prettiest bracelet I've ever seen,' he agreed. 'What charm are you hoping to get when you turn four?'

'A rainbow.'

'Nice!'

'Can you draw rainbows?'

He nodded. 'I'm very good at rainbows.'

'Would you like to draw a rainbow on our painting?'

He took the offer as it was meant—an official seal of approval—and it made his chest expand to the size of a beach ball. 'I'd love to.'

'You were amazing with her today,' Bree said to Noah the next afternoon after glancing around to check on Tilly, who had fallen asleep in her car seat in the back of the car. 'Thank you. It means a lot to me.'

'She's a funny little character.'

'And bossy.'

That made him chuckle. 'She's going to keep you on your toes.'

It was her turn to laugh. 'Absolutely.'

'But you're going to love every minute of it, and so are the rest of us. I'm really looking forward to getting to know her better.'

Her mouth fell open as if his words had taken her by surprise, and then her gaze softened. He forced his gaze back to the road, determined to ignore the hunger snaking through him. 'You're always going to be a part of my life, Bree, which means Tilly is too. I want to form a good relationship with her. We're all going to be there for you, but for her too. None of us will want either of you feeling alone or isolated.'

'Thank you.' She cleared her throat as if his words were in danger of making her cry. 'And I'll tell you something for nothing. I saw today what a wonderful father you're going to make one day. You have the knack.'

His shoulders went back. He had *the knack*?

He glanced into the rear-view mirror at the sleeping child and then at the woman beside him.

He hoped to have a family at some point in the future. A family that loved and looked after each other, supported, nurtured, and on occasion challenged one another. A family that loved and laughed together, and who clung to each other in the tough times.

He glanced at Bree and Tilly again and swallowed, his heart suddenly thumping. He couldn't be thinking…

Not with Bree and Tilly…?

He shook himself, pressed his lips into a tight line. It was just as well he was heading out into the wilderness tomorrow. He needed a timeout to get both hormones and emotions back under control.

Because he couldn't be thinking what he thought he was thinking. Right? It would ruin everything.

CHAPTER NINE

NOAH TRUDGED ALONG the harbour front, hands shoved deep in the pockets of his coat, shoulders hunched, as he stared out at water the colour of mercury—all silver-grey and mauve in the early morning light.

After seven days of trekking through some of the most awe-inspiring scenery he'd ever seen, he should be sick of walking. He should want a rest.

Too much nervous energy flicked through him, though, for that, and it was too early to return to Tina's parents' house. He refused to rock up on their doorstep before nine o'clock. And it was too soon to call on Bree.

He halted and frowned. *Was* it too early to see Bree?

Shaking his head, he forced his feet forward again. He'd been determined to take advantage of the time out the trek had offered him. After the fiasco that had been his wedding, and would've been his marriage if he and Courtney had gone ahead with it, it had become clear that his priorities had needed a major overhaul. The trek had provided the perfect opportunity for him to do that—he'd been off the grid and out of contact.

And yet instead of reassessing his priorities all he'd been able to do was think of Bree.

The fact she was going to become Tilly's guardian.

The fact she planned to relocate to Tasmania.

The fact he knew she'd rather stay in Brisbane than move to Hobart.

All those thoughts had circled around and around in his mind on a continuous loop.

Instead of focussing on fixing all that was wrong with his life, he found himself wanting to fix things for Bree, to make them perfect.

He raked both hands back through his hair. What on earth made him think he could fix Bree's life when he couldn't fix his own?

It was just…he'd always wanted to be her hero. Ever since they were kids.

Making her smile after some childish frustration or playground aggravation had been one of the few things that had made him feel he wasn't completely worthless. They were adults now, though, not children. And yet the impulse remained.

It hadn't just remained. It had *grown*.

Blowing out a breath, he shoved his hands back in his pockets and watched as a yacht threw off its mooring and adjusted its sails to begin its glide downriver to the mouth of the harbour and the open sea.

That was how he should've felt when Courtney had called a halt to their wedding—cast adrift on a cold, lonely ocean. But he hadn't.

Because he hadn't really loved her?

Or because Bree had dragged him along on her road trip and had kept him anchored?

For no reason at all, his heart started thumping—hard—as if it were trying to pound some sense and self-awareness into him. His mouth dried and he couldn't move. Between heartbeats he finally saw what it all meant—his ponderings and the yearning…his vigilance. He finally understood.

He saw how orbiting Bree, as if he were a planet and she his sun, had given his entire life meaning—from the time he was eleven years old until now. It was Bree who'd always been his anchor.

With that realisation came the crystal-clear insight into the real reason he didn't want Bree relocating to Hobart. Not only would he miss her. Not only did the idea leave him feeling cast adrift. But…

No.

He shook his head, panic rising in his throat. *Don't be an idiot*. It didn't mean he was in love with her.

His hands clenched and unclenched, but he couldn't hide from the truth. The thought of losing Bree was a hundred times worse than the thought of losing anyone else in his life.

He'd been so intent on trying to create the picture-perfect life—to prove he was a success and therefore worthy of love and family— that he'd almost missed the fact that his perfect woman had been under his nose all this time.

He'd made a lot of mistakes this past year, but turning his back on his true destiny would be a mistake too far. If there was the slightest possibility that he could be her perfect man too…?

'Hell!'

He braced his hands on his knees and dragged in a breath. If he messed this up… There was so much to lose.

And yet so much to gain.

He straightened and stared at the yacht, which had grown smaller and smaller. Setting his jaw, he turned and headed back the way he'd come.

'I need a research trip,' Tilly shouted the moment she saw Noah later that day. Flying out through the front door and down the path to meet him, she took his hand and squeezed it tight in both her own much smaller ones. Something in his chest squeezed tight too.

He glanced up as Bree tripped down the front path, those milk-chocolate eyes dancing and her scent dredging him as she reached up to kiss his cheek. He wanted to close his eyes and breathe her in.

Correction. He wanted to gather her close and kiss her until neither one of them could think straight.

But one couldn't do that in front of a three-year-old.

He inhaled deeply, but he didn't close his eyes and he didn't gather her close. He needed to take care, move cautiously. He didn't want to do or say anything that would freak Bree out.

She nodded towards Tilly and laughed. 'You've created a monster.'

Tilly frowned. 'I'm not a monster, Auntie Bree!'

'Figure of speech, sweet cheeks,' Bree teased, tickling the little girl, who squealed and raced back to the house where her mother and grandparents waited.

'How was your trek?' Bree asked as they made their way inside.

'Fantastic. Spectacular scenery. Some days it was hard going, but the quiet, the solitude…the grandeur made it all worthwhile. It was a great idea, Bree. Thank you.'

She swung to look at him, eyes wide.

'Fresh air, strenuous exercise, no Internet connection—it was the perfect way to blow away the cobwebs and clear my head.'

Her eyes roved over him and things inside him clenched and burned at the approval he saw in their depths. 'It looks as if it's done you the world of good. You look…'

Her gaze heated and his heart thundered in his chest. 'I look?'

She swallowed. 'Really good.'

She continued to stare at him with wide eyes and a grin started up inside him. He wasn't imagining the hunger in her eyes. Bree still wanted him. She wanted him every bit as much as he wanted her.

It might not be love, but it was something— a start. He could build on it. 'Really good?' he teased, sending her a grin filled with flirtation and devilry.

Hot pink flooded her cheeks and she snapped away. 'Your week away has certainly agreed with you.'

And yet he hadn't felt this alive in the seven days he'd been away. *She* agreed with him.

Tilly tugged on his hand. 'C'mon, Uncle Noah. Come and see my picture.'

He allowed himself to be towed away. Tilly's picture would no doubt clue him in on this research trip she wanted to take. Would it be a kangaroo or a koala? Would he find himself spending tomorrow at the wildlife park again?

He shrugged. He wouldn't mind that one little bit.

'See!'

Tilly held up a picture for him to see. He had no idea what it was, but… 'That's not a kangaroo or a koala,' he hazarded.

'No, silly.' She set the painting down onto the sofa and pointed. 'That's sand and that's a big wave and that's a starfish.'

'Ah, I see.' He sat on the sofa and traced the starfish. 'So let me guess. This research trip you want to take is to the beach?'

She leaned in against his legs, staring up into his face so earnestly it was all he could do not to melt. 'I really, *really* want to go to a big beach with big waves.'

He nodded, pretending to think about it, but he was sold. Glancing at Bree over the top of Tilly's head, he raised an eyebrow and Bree grinned and nodded. 'You know what, kiddo, I think that's a great idea.'

With a cheer, Tilly threw her arms around him.

'Putty,' Bree said with an exaggerated eye roll.

'Wrapped around her little finger,' Tina agreed, wriggling her little finger in a good-natured taunt.

'Why don't we all take a trip to the beach tomorrow?' he suggested. 'One of the guides told me about a beach he loves about an hour north of here. We could take a picnic and make a day of it.'

Tina's face lit up. 'What a great idea.'

Behind her friend's shoulder, Bree smiled at him and mouthed, 'Thank you.'

Any time, he told her silently. Any time he could put that smile on her face, he would.

'We'd like to discuss something with you, Bree,' Corinne started after lunch.

So far their day at the beach had been a roaring success. They had the entire beach, with its long stretch of silvery gold sand and aqua surf, wholly to themselves. They'd paddled—it was too cold to swim—and played beach cricket and built sandcastles to their hearts' content.

The crisp sea air and exercise had put colour in Bree's cheeks and a sparkle in her eyes. Tilly had thrown her whole self into it with so much gusto she'd worn herself out and had fallen asleep on the blanket beside her mother as soon as lunch had been cleared away.

Bree, who had been distributing bottles of water and soft drink among the group, zipped up the cooler bag and turned back to glance at Corinne. 'What would you like to talk about?'

She folded back down to the blanket with an easy grace that had his blood chugging.

'You already know how grateful and happy we are that you're going to be Tilly's guardian.'

'I'm the one who's grateful and happy,' she returned with her trademark big-heartedness.

'And we know that you're fully prepared to move to Hobart and make your life here.'

'Of course.' But some of the sparkle in her eyes dimmed and he wondered if the others saw it too. She sipped her soda before gesturing around. 'Look at everything you have on your doorstep down here. It's not going to be a big sacrifice.'

'But that's just it, honey. We think it is a big sacrifice. And we don't feel right about asking you to make it,' Corinne continued.

Corinne had been nominated as their spokesperson for her tact and her kindness…and because what she was about to propose directly impacted on her and her husband.

'We've come to see over these last ten days or so how much your family means to you.' Corinne smiled. 'We understand that and we know how vital the support of family can be.'

She shared a smile with her husband and daughter. Tina reached out to briefly clasp her mother's hand, and Corinne's eyes filled. 'It's not fair of us to ask you to leave all of that behind.'

Bree, who'd been watching intently, stiffened. 'What are you saying?' she whispered. 'I love Tilly. I'd make any sacrifice necessary for her. Are you telling me you no longer want me to take on the role of Tilly's guardian because you feel bad about asking me to move to Hobart?'

'Heavens, no, honey,' Corinne said, shaking her head.

'Absolutely not,' Tina said.

At the same time as her father said, 'No, no, lass.'

'If there were no other choice, then we would let you make that sacrifice and be even more grateful to you. But what if you could be Tilly's guardian *and* remain in Brisbane?'

Bree's eyes widened. 'Are you considering relocating to Brisbane instead?'

They all nodded.

Bree swung to Noah. 'Did you know about this?'

He shrugged. 'Yes, they told me when I got back from my trek, but—'

'And you didn't think to warn me?'

'Bree—' he reached over to clasp her clenched hands '—everyone needs to make the decision that is best for them. Just listen to what they have to say, okay?'

She searched his face before swinging back to face the others. 'Okay.'

'Well, honey, the thing is… Don and I have been finding the winters here a little too hard in recent years. I know we're not as young as we used to be, but we like to get out and about and be active. For a good four months of the year, though, we're finding ourselves reluctant to brave the weather and not wanting to leave the house. That's no way for us to live.' She sat back, shaking her head. 'These winters are making us feel old.'

'Of course,' Tina took over, 'they haven't wanted to confess any of this to me because they haven't wanted to cause any further upheaval in my life. But the truth is I don't care whether I live in Hobart or Brisbane. Both feel like home to me. I still have friends up north. So if Mum and Dad are going to be happier in Brisbane than here, then I want us to have made the move, like…*yesterday*.'

'Wow,' Bree breathed.

'We've been worried about taking Tina away from her medical team down here. But we've checked and there's a team in Brisbane who come highly recommended and they've agreed to take over Tina's care.'

'That's no biggie.' Tina shrugged. 'We all know, though none of you want to say it out loud, that as my tumour progresses there won't be a lot that can be done for me medically anyway.'

Bree leaned towards her friend. 'Are you a hundred per cent sure about this, Tina? If we're going to be frank then I'll be equally frank. What's really most important here, for all of us, is to make whatever time you have left the best it can be.'

Tears filled Tina's eyes and the tears pouring down Bree's cheeks speared straight into Noah's chest as the women shared a fierce hug.

Tina eventually eased away. She stared down at her sleeping daughter, across to her parents, who were drying their own eyes, and then back at Bree. 'I'm sure. I'm so sure—' she suddenly laughed '—I want to sing and dance.'

Tilly's eyes flew open at her mother's words. She sat up and started to bounce. Noah hadn't known little kids could wake up so fast. 'Can we sing and dance, Mummy? Can we?'

On cue, Bree started to sing 'Dancing Queen' and everyone joined in, Tina and Tilly leaping up to dance.

When Bree held her hand out to Noah in an invitation to dance with her, he didn't hesitate. She starting doing a version of the sixties dance the Swim, so he did his own version of the Chicken dance to make her laugh.

The question that had been hovering in the back of his brain demanding confirmation had been answered.

He wanted Bree. Seeing her, being with her, made him feel alive. She gave him purpose. He wanted to be her hero—he lived to see her smile. It was official—he was in love with Bree Allenby.

The only question that remained now was what was he going to do about it?

'Are you feeling okay with everything? With all the changes Tina and her parents are planning to make?'

It was Saturday and Noah had taken Bree out for drinks in the city centre. They sat on tall stools in a converted warehouse just off Salamanca Place where the iconic weekend markets took place. The bar, with its vaulted ceilings and industrial brickwork, was full of character.

Bree had been hesitant to accept his invitation at first, thinking the less time they spent alone with each other, the better for the time being, but she was glad now that she had. He was just so darn easy to be with.

Buried deep inside her that inconvenient and insistent attraction continued to burn. But when they returned to Brisbane and normality she was confident it would dissolve, and it would be as if it had never existed in the first place. This was just a blip.

Besides, she had a feeling he'd asked her here to reveal his plans for the rest of his…well, vacation, if you could call it that. She had no idea if he planned to share the road trip home or not.

She had no idea if she wanted him to or not.

'Bree?'

She started. 'Sorry, miles away.' She gestured around. 'I love this place.'

'I thought it was about time you had a bit of downtime too.' He stared at her in a way that made her pulse jump. 'It's been an eventful trip, that's for sure.'

That made her laugh. 'In more ways than one.' She met his gaze. 'But in answer to your question, I am feeling more optimistic, more hopeful, more…blessed than I think I have any right to feel.'

'You deserve all of that and more.'

The warmth of his gaze sent a corresponding warmth zipping through her, but it wasn't the kind of heat that made her uneasy. It was just Noah being his usual generous and protective self.

During the course of her teenage years—and later as well—her brothers' protectiveness had often irked her. But Noah's never had. He'd always been careful not to impinge on her freedom or to let her think he thought her incompetent or incapable of making a wise decision.

He'd only ever wanted the best for her as she did for him.

'Do you truly think Tina and her parents want to move to Brisbane? Or do you think they're making a sacrifice for me? Or maybe Tilly?'

She'd move heaven and earth to provide Tina with everything she wanted and needed to make whatever time she had left happy and content. Sure, relocating to Hobart would've been a wrench, but she considered it a sacrifice worth making if it would make Tina and her parents happy.

'All of them are prepared to make sacrifices for Tilly's welfare, Bree, just like you. Don't discount that. It's at the heart of everything. It's the issue that everyone sees as the most important one. As they should.'

He glanced at her over the rim of his glass as he sipped his beer. A boutique craft beer he'd pronounced, 'Wickedly good.'

She sipped the glass of Shiraz he'd bought for her, relishing its deep, peppery plumminess. 'Are you saying they think Tilly will be happier in Brisbane?'

'Of course she will. That's a no-brainer. Tilly will be happiest where she's surrounded by people who love her. Beyond her current circle, in Brisbane she'll also have your parents, your brothers and me. That means five extra people, beyond her mother, grandparents and you, who are going to embrace her and form part of her family. How can she not benefit from all that love?'

He made it sound idyllic.

'And then there's your wider circle of friends who'll be a support to you too. You have girlfriends with children—I'm seeing play dates, the comparing of notes on child development, and discussions about the pros and cons of various schools.'

That made her laugh. Her life was going to change in the most dramatic fashion, but... It didn't frighten her as much as it had at the start of this trip. Noah made it sound as if she could really, truly do this. His belief in her filled her with confidence and a newly found sense of self-assurance.

He covered her hand with his. 'What are you really worried about?'

She squeezed his hand before dragging hers from his hold. His touch sent an unsettling surge of desire through her, making all the fine hairs on her arms lift—as if they were all reaching out towards him.

She would *not* do anything foolish. She would *not* do anything impulsive. She would *not* act on this attraction and ruin everything.

She was starting to feel that she could finally become the kind of daughter her parents deserved, the sister her brothers deserved, not to mention the kind of friend Noah deserved.

Most importantly, though, she felt as if she could become the kind of mother that Tilly deserved—someone steady and reliable, unselfish and responsible, someone level-headed and balanced.

Oh, and the chance to do that on her home turf…

She closed her eyes. She was unbelievably blessed. She didn't need any more. She'd be content with what she had.

'Bree?'

And she had to keep her mind on track!

She ran a finger around the rim of her glass. 'I guess I don't want them to be sad at all they're leaving behind. I don't want them to regret this decision.' She met his gaze. 'I don't want them to be…less happy.'

The fact that the time Tina had left was so finite was hard enough for them all to deal with. She didn't want to add to that stress or sadness.

'What if I told you that I've spoken to each and every one of them on the subject?'

Her gaze speared back to his. She searched his face but saw nothing other than a frank openness. 'Have you?'

He nodded.

'And?'

He looked as if he wanted to take her hand again and her heart crashed about in her chest, but at the last moment he wrapped his hands around his beer, and she pulled her hands into her lap.

'Of course, they're going to miss the friends they've made here. And they have favourite places here that they love.'

Her heart clenched. She couldn't—wouldn't—ask them to give that up.

'But there's so much excitement too about returning to Brisbane that more than makes up for it.'

She searched his face again.

'Tina calls it going home.'

That smile of his flashed out and she couldn't help smiling back. 'Really?'

He nodded. 'Corinne and Don are looking forward to seeing old friends.'

He stared down into his beer, but the gold in his eyes flashed when he glanced back up at her, and it made it hard to catch her breath.

'They've not said much but apparently the winters here have become hell on Corinne's eczema and Don's bad knee. They both have arthritis. They truly long for a warmer climate. I can assure you, hand on heart, this move is bringing far more positives for them than negatives.'

She sagged, the last of her doubts disappearing. She reached across to grip his hand. 'Thank you. Thank you for checking all of that with them.' She didn't doubt for a moment that he'd done it because he'd sensed her concerns.

He shrugged. 'I just want everyone to be happy.'

He had the biggest heart of any man she'd ever met. 'I'm so glad you were with me on this trip, Noah. It's been a life-changing time and you've helped so much. Without your support...' She shook her head, unable to conceive what her world would be without it.

'You mean that?'

'Of course I do.' But something in his tone made her mouth go dry.

'I realised something startling when I returned from my trek, and yet, in hindsight, I guess it shouldn't have been all that surprising.'

Prickles of awareness raced from his palm to hers, and then to every far-flung corner of her body. Her breasts grew heavy, her stomach softened, and her lips parted in an attempt to drag air into cramped lungs. She wanted to wrench her hand away, but it seemed rude...unsupportive. So she gritted her teeth and left it where it was.

Noah had helped her so much over the last three weeks. She couldn't be so ungracious as to cut him short when he wanted to discuss something of personal importance with her.

She had no idea what his epiphany had been, but she could tell it meant a lot to him. She swallowed. She couldn't smile, that was beyond her, but she could listen. 'What did you realise after your week in the wilderness?'

He stared at her with dark eyes and her heart thudded harder and faster when he didn't immediately answer. She leaned towards him. 'Noah, you're starting to worry me.'

He leaned in closer too until his warm male scent, so familiar to her, dredged her senses. Those hazel eyes with their flashes of gold should've been familiar too, but she'd never seen that expression in them before. She battled the temptation to reach for him.

Don't ruin everything.

'I realised, Bree—' those eyes bored into hers '—that I'm in love with you.'

She froze.

'I think I've always been in love with you, I was just too blind to see it.'

She flinched away. 'No!'

'Yes.'

'Noah, this is crazy. Three weeks ago you were getting married to another woman! This trip has been an emotional roller coaster of a ride and—'

'I'm not on the rebound, Bree.' His lips twisted. 'Except, perhaps from my own stupidity. Courtney didn't break my heart. And I didn't break hers. We never had that kind of power over each other.'

She couldn't be hearing this. It couldn't be happening.

'You made me realise how hung up I still was about my past, and forced me to face the real reason I wanted to marry Courtney...and what a mistake it would've been if we'd gone through with it.' He shook his head. 'I won't blame her if she never forgives me.'

Bree would, but that was not what she had to focus on at the moment.

'The fact remains—I wasn't in love with her.'

But that didn't mean he was in love with Bree instead. She had to *fix* this.

'I couldn't love any other woman when my heart so wholly and totally belongs to you. I want to build a life with you. I want—'

'*No.*'

He paled. Her single word seemed to echo in the sudden silence that stretched between them. Noah's pallor speared into her heart, but she shook her head and did all she could to harden it.

'How can you dismiss it so quickly? How can you treat my declaration as if it means nothing?' His eyes throbbed with darkness. 'Why won't you take a moment to search your own heart? To take a look deep inside yourself and consider—'

'There's nothing to consider. Hell, Noah, you've been so set on creating this wonderful idyllic vision of a family with Courtney and now you've transferred all of that onto Tilly and me. I know you admire what I'm doing, and I know Tilly has squirmed her way into your heart, but as soon as you return to Brisbane and the real world you're going to see how mistaken you are.'

His mouth became a thin white line. 'Do you remember talking to me about heartbreak on the first night of the road trip? Do you remember how you described it to me?'

She remembered every damn word.

'What you didn't say was how there's absolutely no light or joy in the world when the person you love isn't near or when you discover they don't want you. That it's an effort to put one foot in front of the other. And that some hurts go too deep even for tears.'

He dragged a hand back through his hair. 'I know I've been blind, and I know I've been an idiot, but I've finally worked it out. Don't discount it simply because you're afraid or because you have so much going on in your life or because you think you can't trust me. I would *never* do anything to hurt you. You have to know that.'

Not intentionally, he wouldn't.

'After the conversation we had the first afternoon of our farm stay, Bree… Do you honestly think I'd try and manipulate you in an attempt to gain my mythic idyllic marriage? Do you think I've learned nothing these last few weeks?' He stared. 'You have to know you can trust me.'

She dragged in a breath, refusing to let his words seduce her. She forced her mind to her family, forced herself to remember the shocked expressions on her parents' faces when they'd bailed her from jail—the devastation her mother hadn't been able to keep from her eyes when she'd learned Bree had been arrested for drug possession. The fury and outrage in not only her father's eyes but her brothers' as well when they'd sat through Otis's court hearing when she'd had to give evidence. She'd known it hadn't been directed at her, but if it hadn't been for her they wouldn't have had to suffer through all of that. She couldn't bear to see any of them ever look at her like that again.

She would *not* mess up again.

Lifting her chin, she wrapped determination about her like a barricade. 'Hasn't it occurred to you that in becoming involved with me you'd be risking your relationship with my entire family?' She struggled to get her head around it. 'For heaven's sake, you're in business with Ryder. And I know how much my parents mean to you.'

On the table, his hands clenched to fists. He

leaned towards her. 'All of it is worth risking for you. Can't you see? Without you, none of it matters.'

Everything inside her yearned and strained towards him. He looked so true and sincere...and so damn tempting. She beat it back down. 'It's not worth it to me!'

His head rocked back. His face turned grey. With a muttered oath he lifted his beer to his lips and drained it. He set it back down with a snap, his eyes flashing. 'So you're going to be a coward?'

What on earth...?

'I'm not Otis, Bree.' He gave a harsh laugh. 'It seems I've been an idiot *again*. While I might've moved out of my old way of looking at things, and doing what you urged me to do—looking towards the future rather than remaining stuck in the past—you're refusing to take your own advice.'

'I don't know what you're talking about.' She wanted to scoff, but her throat had grown too tight and her voice emerged small and choked.

'You're too frightened of making another mistake to risk your heart again in case you screw up.'

'So what if I am? I owe it to my family to not be that screw-up.'

'But what do you owe yourself? You're simply hiding behind your family as an excuse. Because you're afraid.' He leaned in close. 'But I've seen the way you look at me, Bree. I *know* you want me.'

Heat flooded her cheeks. She'd thought she'd hidden it, kept it from him. 'Lust isn't love, Noah. You know that.'

'Ever since we kissed in Melbourne, it's taken all of my control not to haul you into my arms and repeat the experience.'

Her heart hammered up into her throat. 'Don't you dare kiss me again.'

'And at least I'm honest enough to admit it.' He sat back, his nostrils flaring. 'I want all of you, Bree—your heart, not just your body. I'm honest enough to admit that as well. Even if you're intent on sticking your head in the sand.'

'What I want,' she said through gritted teeth, 'is for things to go back to the way they were before. I just want us to be friends.' Her heart thumped all the way up into her throat. She swallowed it down. 'Please tell me that's possible.' She couldn't keep the pleading note out of her voice.

He rose, nodding at their empty glasses. 'Ready to go?'

Panic fluttered through her. 'You're saying we can't be friends?'

'I want more than friendship from you. It was

you who made me believe I deserved more than what I'd been willing to settle for. You can't quibble now when I refuse to settle for less.'

What did that mean in practical terms?

He stared at her, his eyes dark with pain—pain she'd caused. Everything inside her protested. Her eyes burned and her throat ached. But surely this was better than risking his relationship with her entire family? When he returned to Brisbane, he'd see that she'd been right.

'I think it'll be best if we don't see each other for a while.'

He couldn't mean that. 'How long is a while?'

'How long did it take for you to get over Otis?'

No!

He couldn't stay away that long. She had to find a way to make things right. She made herself breathe through the panic. When he returned to Brisbane, he'd see that she was right.

And then things would return to normal.

But no matter how much she told herself that, the fear continued to pound at her. The fear that she might've lost Noah forever.

CHAPTER TEN

'I HEARD YOU come in last night.' Tina glanced up from the breakfast table where she sipped a coffee. Tilly was glued to the TV where she watched cartoons in the allotted half an hour TV time Tina gave her each morning. 'It wasn't exactly a late night.'

Bree helped herself to coffee from the pot. 'I hate to disappoint, but my days of painting the town red are long past.' She stifled a yawn. 'Besides, I had a headache.' A headache that went by the name of Noah. And she didn't want to talk about it. She slid into the seat opposite. 'Hence the early night.'

Not that she'd managed much sleep. She'd tossed and turned until the wee small hours, searching her mind to try and make things right with Noah. The thought of not seeing him for however long it took him to get over this crazy notion that he was in love with her tormented her.

Whenever she'd closed her eyes, the pain that had raked his face when she'd told him—

She swallowed and stared down into her coffee. His darkness and despair when she'd told him she didn't love him… Even now it tore her to shreds from the inside out. She'd ached to find relief in tears, but they'd refused to come.

'You do look a bit pale.' Tina surveyed her critically. 'It's been a bit of an emotional roller coaster for all of us these last few days, Bree. If you're having second thoughts—'

'No!' She straightened so swiftly coffee sloshed over the sides of her cup. She grabbed a wad of tissues from her pocket and soaked up the spill, before reaching across and grabbing her friend's hand. 'No second thoughts, I swear. I just…'

Tina's gaze raked her face and Bree sensed she had her friend's full attention. 'You just…?'

Bree pulled in a breath. 'Are you really, truly one hundred per cent sure you want to move back to Brisbane?'

Tina laughed, her relief evident in her sudden smile. 'So *that's* what's been bothering you.'

That and Noah. But she didn't say that out loud.

'Oh, Bree, please stop worrying. There was a part of me that always knew you'd eventually move back to Brisbane.'

There was?

'It's your home. And now I'm getting the chance to have a peek at what Tilly's future life is going to look like.' She pressed both hands to her chest. 'I feel so fortunate to be able to do that. I know this is going to sound crazy, but—'

She broke off to pull in a deep breath. 'If I'm there at the beginning of Tilly's life in Brisbane, maybe she'll always feel that I'm close and a part of things, even when I'm no longer there. In the meantime, I get to see your family forging relationships with my little girl and growing to love her. Oh, Bree, don't doubt for a moment that this is what I want.'

The two women hugged—a hug of solidarity and sisterhood.

'Okay.' Bree drew back and made herself grin, reminding herself of Tina's 'Only happy thoughts' motto. 'I can stop worrying about that, then. Now we just have to work out the logistics.'

'Noah's already on it.'

She tried not to flinch at the mention of his name. 'What do you mean?'

'Did he not mention it last night? He's flown out to Brisbane this morning.'

Her mouth dried. He'd gone already?

Tina rolled her eyes. 'He made some transparent excuse about how he's been wanting to invest in real estate for some time now—grilled me and my parents about our ideal homes—and has gone off to, quote, *scope them out*.'

He was buying houses for Tina and her parents?

'He plans to buy them and then wants us to use them for as long as we want, rent-free.'

Bree huffed out a laugh. That sounded like Noah—generous to a fault.

'I'm more than happy to let him do the legwork and take the stress out of the move, but we'll be paying our way.'

Tina looked carefree and happy, and Bree blessed Noah a hundred times over. But...

He'd left without saying goodbye. And she didn't know when she'd see him again.

Staring out of Tina's big glass sliding doors, she could see that the sun shone, but in her mind storm clouds had turned the world dark.

'Of course, we have you to thank for all of that.'

That snapped her back. 'Me?'

'That guy has always done whatever he could to make your life easier, Bree. And we're reaping the benefits.'

'What are you talking about?'

Tina rolled her eyes. '*Puhlease!* Noah has always been your white knight. Ever since Dougie Green called you a prissy princess crybaby when we were nine and Noah sat on him so you could draw glitter hearts all over Dougie's face before he had to go to football training.'

The memory had a laugh shooting from her. It had taken Dougie a long time to live that one down and he'd never called her names again.

'Noah has always had your back, Bree.'

And just like that, everything fell into place. Noah did have her back, just as she always had his. When he'd said he loved her, he'd meant it. He'd never play those kinds of games with her, she meant too much to him. And falling in love with him didn't make her a screw-up. It made her the smartest damn person on the planet!

She grabbed Tina's shoulders. 'I've made the biggest mistake! Last night Noah told me he loved me, but I told him it was impossible and that I didn't love him.'

'You did *what*? But you do!'

'I know! I mean I didn't realise it last night, but I do now.' Bree dragged both hands back through her hair. 'But he laid it on me without warning. I thought he was going on his trek to sort his head out and…and—'

She stared at her friend, appalled at how much she'd misunderstood *everything*. 'I had no idea that him and me, as a couple, was on the radar or…even a possibility.'

'He finally saw what has been plain to the rest of us.' Tina shook her head, 'Since, like, for *ever*.'

'Then why am I the last to work it out?' Bree demanded.

'Because you've been working so hard at being Little Miss Perfect.'

There was love in Tina's smile, not judgement. Bree sank back down into her chair. 'I was a coward.'

'You're not a coward, Bree. He took you by surprise and scared the bejesus out of you.'

'I was a coward,' she repeated, before glancing over at Tilly. 'That's not the kind of role model I want to be.' She wanted to teach Tilly to fight for the things she wanted, to have courage.

She swung back to Tina. She loved Noah with every fibre of her being. 'I need to make this right. *Now.* I have to see him as soon as I possibly can.'

'Go and pack an overnight bag. Quick! I'm getting you on the next flight out of Hobart.'

Bree leapt to her feet and started towards her bedroom. She swung back, massaging her temples. 'What day is it?'

'Sunday.'

She and Tina stared at each other. 'Sunday night family dinner,' they both said at the same time.

Every instinct she had told her he'd be there tonight. He'd want the solace of family. And she'd move heaven and earth to make sure she was there too.

* * *

Bree shoved a handful of notes at the taxi driver, with a hurried, 'Keep the change,' before grabbing her bag and racing to the front door of her family home. On Sunday evenings the door was never locked.

Dropping her bag in the entry foyer, she hurtled into the dining room.

Every head swung around at her abrupt entrance.

Including Noah's.

She pressed a hand to her chest and sent up a prayer of thanks that he was there, before she registered that he'd been in the process of rising to his feet with an, 'I'm sorry, but I have to go.'

She took a step towards him. 'Please don't go,' she whispered, her heart hammering.

He fell down into his chair as if the shock of seeing her had robbed his legs of strength.

'Honey, we weren't expecting you for another week at least,' her mother said, 'and—'

'Something came up,' Bree inserted quickly to forestall the volley of questions. She then pointed around the table at her family and then pressed a finger to her lips. 'I know this is going to be really hard for you all,' she said, 'but not a word.'

Dragging a breath into lungs that didn't want to work, she met Noah's burning gaze, the love gathering beneath her breastbone making her ache.

She wanted to race across and throw herself into his arms, press her lips to his and just touch him. She forced herself to remain where she was. He might not want her to touch him and how could she blame him after her coldness last night?

'What are you doing here, Bree?' he finally said.

He looked pale and the strain about his eyes made her want to cry. She couldn't stop from walking around the table to him and touching a hand to his cheek.

He'd pushed his chair back and she dropped to her knees beside him and took his hands in hers. 'I'm so sorry, Noah,' she choked out. 'Last night I panicked and—'

'It's okay, Bree.' His words emerged stiff but resolute. 'You can't help the way you feel.'

She saw then exactly how much he did love her, because even now, while in the depths of his own pain and despair, he was trying to make things easy for her. She shook her head. 'It's not okay, because last night I lied—to you *and* to myself.'

His gaze speared to hers. Hope burned to life in the hazel of his eyes, but he quickly annihilated it.

She couldn't be too late. *She couldn't.* Her life would be dust and ashes without this man. She wasn't letting him go without a fight.

She lifted her chin. 'I love you, Noah. I probably always have. It's probably the real reason I loathed Courtney…and why I gave every girlfriend you've ever had the derogatory moniker of Noah's Nymphette.' She grimaced. 'Not exactly progressive of me, huh?'

His eyes narrowed and he searched her face as if he suspected her of lying.

'I love you, Noah,' she repeated, because she'd never get sick of saying it.

He shook his head. 'This isn't the way to make things right, Bree.' He spoke gently, but his words were laced in steel. 'Sacrificing yourself to keep the peace and make sure everyone is happy is not the answer.'

Her chin hitched up even higher. 'I'm not sacrificing myself! I'm trying to win my happy ever after. Last night when you told me you loved me, I panicked. All I could see were the million and one ways I could screw us up…and not just us.' She gestured around the table to encompass her family.

She tightened her grip on his hands. 'But I was focussing on the wrong things. What I should've been focussing on were the million and one ways we make sense. I'm your champion and you're my hero. Us being together is right…and perfect.'

He blinked.

'This morning I realised that being with you was worth taking any and every risk necessary.

So...' She swallowed, starting to run out of steam, achingly aware that her entire family was staring at her with the kind of expressions that screamed *train wreck*. 'So I came here as soon as I could. To tell you I love you; to try and fix things.'

Had she missed her chance with him? Had he closed himself off so completely from her because of the stupid things she'd said last night?

She met his gaze, not sure she'd ever felt more vulnerable in her life. 'Please tell me I'm not too late. Because there's something else I forgot to tell you about heartbreak—when you hurt the person you love it's as if you've stabbed a knife into your own chest. When I think of last night and the way I turned away from you—the things I said—it's a hundred times worse than when Otis betrayed me.'

She swallowed back the sob that pressed against her throat. 'I'll understand if you want nothing to do with me now. I only wish I could take away all the pain that I caused you, and take it onto myself. You're the best man I know, Noah, and you don't deserve anything but love and happiness.'

His gaze searched hers, those eyes dark and penetrating. His nostrils flared. 'You mean it.'

He uttered the words so quietly she had to strain to hear them. She nodded.

His lips swooped down then and captured hers in a fierce kiss that stole her breath.

He eased away, his eyes just as fierce as his kiss. 'You know I'm going to demand everything from you, Bree? I'm going to ask for it all.'

'Which is just as well, because I don't want anything less from you either. This is forever,' she added when he stood and drew her to her feet.

'It's forever,' he agreed, a light flashing in his eyes making the gold flecks in their depths sparkle, his mouth curving into the widest of smiles that sent her pulse dancing.

With a whoop, he picked her up and swung her around, and it felt as if they were both flying. She wrapped her arms about his neck and threw her head back. 'I love you, Noah!'

He set her on her feet again, his love shining from his eyes. 'I love you, Bree.'

She kissed him, a kiss full of jubilation, and when she eased back a moment later she became aware of the dining room, and her family…and Sunday night family dinner.

Everyone stared at her and Noah with a mixture of astonishment, confusion and a strange blend of denial and approval. 'Not a word,' she told them. 'I don't care what any of you think. This is the smartest decision I have ever made. You'll see. And while we're on the subject I don't want you bailing Noah up or giving him any grief about this.' She glared at her brothers. 'If he ever changes his mind about me—'

'Not going to happen,' Noah said, shaking his head.

'Whatever happens,' Bree stressed over the top of him, 'Noah is a member of this family, and he'll always be a member of this family. I want everyone here to remember that.'

Her mother dabbed at her eyes and smiled at them mistily. Her father cleared his throat—once, twice, and merely nodded. Blake and Ryder glanced at each other and broke into grins. 'About time,' they said in tandem.

'My champion indeed,' Noah murmured, staring down at her with a compelling mixture of tenderness and heat. 'And I plan to always be your hero, Bree. What do you want right now?' He smiled. 'What feat can I perform for you?'

It was spoken in jest, but Bree knew exactly what she wanted. 'I want you to take me into the garden where we can have a little privacy so you can kiss me senseless.'

So he did.

A long while later she was sprawled on his lap on a garden bench. She reached up to touch his face. 'I'm so sorry about last night. I'm sorry I panicked and couldn't see what seems so obvious to me now.'

He pressed a finger to her lips. 'I'm the one who should be apologising. I gave you no warning whatsoever what was in my heart prior to Saturday night. I just blurted it out and expected you to be on the same page. I should've realised sooner how much it would frighten you. I should've known how worried you'd be that if things didn't work out between us I'd lose your family. Because you know how important your family is to me.'

He touched her face. 'Dearest Bree, I should've taken the time to woo you and win you over—to listen to your fears and then work through them with you to show you they were groundless. I should've given you time to adjust rather than storming off. I should've proved to you that you're more important than anybody or anything in the world by sticking around and fighting for you.'

'I should've been braver.'

'You couldn't be braver if you tried,' he said, seizing her lips in a kiss of pure exaltation that made her blood dip and swoop as if she were on a fairground ride—filling her with excitement and exhilaration. And joy.

He lifted his head, his fingers caressing her face. 'My beautiful, brave Bree.' And then he kissed her with such tenderness she melted.

When he lifted his head some time later, she

had to blink the tears from her eyes. 'I can't wait until we're *alone* alone,' she whispered.

The gold sparks in his eyes flared.

'Oh!' She sat up a little straighter. 'You were leaving. When I first arrived, you were about to go. Am I keeping you from something?' He'd been away from work for a good three weeks. There were probably a million things he had to do, hundreds of matters demanding his attention.

His low laugh had her very centre softening. She wanted to beg him to laugh like that again.

'I was about to head to the airport to catch the next flight back to Hobart. I was going to find you and tell you that I loved you but respected your feelings on the subject…and then I was going to do anything and everything to win your heart.'

She pressed a hand to his chest, awed that this amazing man loved her. Beneath her palm his heart beat hard and strong. 'You were coming back for me?'

He nodded.

She wondered if it was possible to feel happier than she felt right at this very moment.

'You know I want to marry you, Bree?'

'Of course.' She feigned nonchalance, as if that fact were self-evident, but a thousand fireworks went off inside her.

'I think you'd love to have Tina as your maid of honour and Tilly as flower girl.'

He was right, but that meant… 'You want to get married sooner rather than later, huh?'

'I'll understand if you want to wait. The press will have a field day, and the speculation will be…trying.'

'Only if they can drag themselves away from speculating about Courtney partying on that Greek billionaire's yacht.'

He grinned. 'You saw that?'

'Read it on the plane.' She shrugged. 'I hope she's having fun.' She found herself wishing Courtney the same kind of happiness she'd found. 'Noah, I don't care what the press says. I love you.'

'And I love you.'

'Then I propose we get married when we want, live our lives on our own terms, and be happy. What do you say?'

'I say that's an excellent plan.'

And then he kissed her with an enthusiasm that left her in no doubt how much he approved of her plan.

EPILOGUE

Two years later

'WE NEED TO go on a research trip,' Tilly announced.

Noah glanced up from the picture he was drawing. Tilly's voice had taken on that too-innocent edge and he had to suppress a grin. 'Why? What do you need to study in more detail?'

She turned her picture around. 'Do you know what that is?'

He'd got much getter at this game during the fourteen months Tilly had been living with him and Bree. He and Tilly spent a lot of time drawing together. It was their thing. Especially in that awkward hour after dinner and before bedtime, like now.

He pursed his lips. 'It looks like a dog.'

Tilly frowned. 'But it's not very good. It's supposed to be a baby dog—a puppy.'

'So...we need to find some puppies, is that

what you're telling me? So you can learn to draw them better?'

Tilly nodded so hard he was afraid she'd make herself dizzy. Over the top of her head, he and Bree shared a secret smile.

'I guess I better see what I can manage,' he agreed. 'I'll put my thinking cap on.'

He and Bree had bought Tilly a puppy and were planning to give it to her at the end of her birthday party tomorrow. Tomorrow when she turned six! The last couple of years had flown by.

Tilly launched herself into his arms. 'I love you, Daddy.'

'I love you too, Princess.'

Eight months ago Tilly had announced to him and Bree that she wanted to call them Mummy and Daddy, like all the kids in her class called their parents Mummy and Daddy. 'Because you are,' she'd said. 'You are my mummy and my daddy.'

The memory could still make his chest swell and bring a lump to his throat.

She raced over to Bree and pressed a kiss to Bree's baby bump. 'It's my birthday party to-morrow, Baby. If you were here you could have some of my unicorn cake and play games and wear a princess dress too.'

She climbed up into Bree's lap and Bree snug-gled her close. His heart gave a giant thump. His wife was the most amazing mother. She and Tilly adored one another, and he knew that Bree would adore whoever else came along in the future with that same ferocity.

He glanced at that baby bump and his heart expanded. He'd never known it was possible for a man to be this happy.

Tilly bit her lip. 'My party is going to be fun, isn't it?'

Their daughter was a worrier. 'You bet,' Bree said with so much confidence, Noah couldn't help but smile. 'Just you wait and see. It's going to be a huge success. How can it be otherwise when Nanna and Grandma are in charge of the food, Poppy and Granddad are in charge of the party decorations, and Uncle Ryder and Uncle Blake are in charge of the party games?'

Tilly's face cleared.

'What's more,' Bree added, 'you have the best princess dress in the world to wear and there's going to be a unicorn cake.'

'And I have Mummy's fairy charm.' Tilly held up her wrist, the dangling charms on her charm bracelet twinkling.

'And that definitely has to be a good luck sign. Your party is going to be sprinkled with fairy dust.'

Tilly nodded, happy again.

Tina, before she'd become too sick, had purchased a charm for Tilly's every birthday until she'd turned eighteen. It was Tilly's most treasured possession, and it had become a tradition to give the charm to her the night before her birthday.

When Tilly was in bed, Noah made Bree a chamomile tea, grabbed a soda for himself and they headed out to their back deck with its view of the Brisbane River. It flowed by steady and calm, reflecting back the night sky with its three-quarter moon and myriad stars.

Setting her mug to the table, Bree walked over to lean against the railing. She'd been a little quieter tonight than usual.

'Tired?' he asked, walking over to slide his arms around her waist and pull her back against him.

'A little.'

'You should be worn to a frazzle with all of this party organisation.'

That made her laugh. 'I've hardly had to lift a finger. Everyone else has insisted on doing the heavy lifting.'

'They love it,' he told her. And they wanted her to take it easy at the moment, to take care of herself.

She laughed again. 'They do.'

As Noah had always suspected, Bree's entire family had embraced Tilly and her family as their own. The whole clan was looking forward to tomorrow's party with the kind of glee generally reserved for grand final day and family weddings.

Which immediately had him flashing back to his and Bree's wedding nineteen months ago. It had been small and unassuming, and it couldn't have been more perfect.

'How's the training going with your new second in command?' With her upcoming maternity leave looming in four months' time, Bree was training up her assistant to take over while she was away.

Bree had grown the entire physio and dietetics side of operations at Fitness Ark from the ground up and it had proved successful beyond all of their wildest expectations. The franchise continued to go from strength to strength.

'She's an absolute wonder. We want to keep her, Noah. She's too valuable an asset to the company to let someone else poach her.'

Which was what had happened with her previous assistant. He made a mental note to discuss a pay rise for her with Ryder and the accountant next week.

She rested her head against his shoulder. 'The doctor called me in for an appointment today.'

He immediately stiffened.

'Relax.' She chuckled. 'Everything is absolutely perfect.'

She placed her hands over the ones he'd spread possessively across her expanding belly.

'Then why did the doc want to see you?'

She turned, her arms going around his neck. 'There was something in my previous scan that puzzled her. She wanted to do another ultrasound just to make sure.'

He frowned, but her eyes were shining and not a trace of worry lined her face. She was so beautiful she stole his breath. 'Make sure of what?' he murmured, resisting the urge to kiss her.

'To make sure she was counting the right number of arms and legs.'

He stared, not understanding.

'Today's scan confirmed it.' Her eyes danced and her smile was as wide as the sky. 'Noah, we're having twins!'

He could feel his jaw drop and his eyes widen. 'Twins?' he parroted.

She nodded, excitement radiating from every pore. She cupped his face. 'Tell me you're happy rather than freaked out.'

With a whoop, he picked her up and swung her around. Setting her on her feet again, he bent and kissed her with all the feeling in his overflowing heart.

'Oh!' She clutched his arms when he finally lifted his head, her eyes dazed. 'Perfect response.'

The pulse at the base of her throat fluttered and that familiar heat coursed through him. 'I'm married to you, we have a daughter, and now we're going to have twins…life can't get any more perfect.'

She reached up to cup his face, her eyes soft and full of love. 'You deserve every ounce of happiness and every good thing this world has to offer you.'

'You really think so?' some devil made him ask.

Her eyes widened. 'Of course.'

He swung her up in his arms. 'Does that mean I can talk you into an early night? That would *definitely* add to my current happiness.'

She pressed her lips to his cheek. 'I thought you'd never ask. An early night sounds perfect.'

He strode inside with the woman he loved in his arms, determined to show her exactly how perfect he thought her.

* * * * *